SHORT STORY

INTERNATIONAL

**Tales by the World's
Great Contemporary Writers
Presented Unabridged**

D1488080

All selections in
Short Story International
are published full and
unabridged.

Editor
Sylvia Tankel

Associate Editor
Erik Sandberg-Diment

Contributing Editor
John Harr

Assistant Editors
Mildred Butterworth
Debbie Kaufman
Kirsten Hammerle

Art Director
Charles W. Walker

Circulation Director
Nat Raboy

Production Director
Michael Jeffries

Business Manager
John O'Connor

Publisher
Sam Tankel

Volume 13, Number 74, June 1989.
Short Story International (USPS 375-970)
Copyright © by International Cultural
Exchange 1989. Printed in U.S.A. All rights
reserved. Reproduction in whole or in part
prohibited. Second-class postage paid at
Great Neck, N.Y. 11022 and at additional
mailing offices. **Editorial offices: P.O. Box
405, Great Neck, N.Y. 11022.** Enclose
stamped, self-addressed envelope with
submission. One year (six issues) subscription
for U.S., U.S. possessions $22, Canada $24
(US), other countries $25 (US). Single copy
price $4.45. **For subscriptions and
address changes write to Short Story
International, P.O. Box 405, Great
Neck, N.Y. 11022.** *Short Story
International* is published bimonthly by
International Cultural Exchange, 6 Sheffield
Road, Great Neck, N.Y. 11021. Postmaster
please send Form 3579 to P.O. Box 405,
Great Neck, N.Y. 11022.

Table of Contents

Copyrights and acknowledgments

We wish to express deep thanks to the authors, publishers, translators and literary agents for their permission to publish the stories in this issue.

"One Winter in Wallawood" by Margot Titcher originally appeared in the *Journal*. Copyright 1987 Margot Titcher. "The Sand Fox" by Guo Xuebo appeared in *Chinese Literature*, 1987. Translation by Yu Fanqin. By permission. "The Princess" by Irena Ioannidou Adamidou. Translation by Christine Georgiadou. Copyright Irena Ioannidou Adamidou. "Odessa" by Alex Auswaks. Copyright 1989 Alex Auswaks. "The Bore" by E.G. Chipulina, 1989. "The Swim" by Dezső Kosztolányi appeared in *The New Hungarian Quarterly*, 1985. Translation by Eszter Molnár. By permission of Artisjus. "Eye-Witness" by Dina Mehta appeared in *The Illustrated Weekly of India*. Copyright Dina Mehta. "Snow in Paris" by Sitor Situmorang from *From Surabaya to Armaggeddon: Indonesian Short Stories*, edited and translated by Harry Aveling. Copyright © Heinemann Educational Books (Asia) Ltd. By permission. "Crumbs" by Amnon Shamosh appeared in *Present Tense*. Translation by Barbara Benavie. Copyright Amnon Shamosh. "The Folly" by Tariq Rahman originally appeared in *The Frontier Post*, 1986. By permission. "The Journey" from *Little Ironies: Stories of Singapore* by Catherine Lim. Published by Heinemann Educational Books (Asia) Ltd. Copyright © 1978 Catherine Lim. "The Hunt" by Joseph Patron, 1989. "Night Shift" from *Gece Vardujasi* by Fakir Baykurt. Translation by Joseph S. Jacobson, 1989. "Who's to Say This Isn't Love?" by William Pitt Root originally appeared in *TriQuarterly*. Copyright © William Pitt Root 1983. "Dancing on the Radio" from *The London Embassy* by Paul Theroux. Published by Houghton Mifflin Company, Boston. Copyright © Cape Cod Scriveners Company. Reprinted by permission of the publisher and Aitken & Stone Ltd.

Photo Credits: Paul Theroux by Nancy Maguire. William Pitt Root by Pamela Uschuk.

"What goes on in that sharp brain of his?"

One Winter in Wallawood

BY MARGOT TITCHER

WEDNESDAY, 14th June

What a day! It started well enough. The children took to the new number cards with enthusiasm, though Fred Phillips peeked at the answers on the flip side. Poor Fred, his first time ahead of the class! I didn't have the heart to let on that I was alert to his ruse. The novelty kept them engrossed for the entire Arithmetic period. And no black looks through the glass of the partition wall from Mrs. Finch of 1B. How does that woman make her group so well-behaved?

When the disruption came, it was from a totally surprising source. I mean, one would have expected it from Freddie considering his limited span of attention, or from Cherie with a jiggling request to "leave the room," but the rumble of rollers in their track, as the sliding door slammed back, caught us all off guard.

It was the Head—old pouter pigeon Patterson—his chest puffed up with conceit, and straining inside the three-piece blue that never seemed to leave his back, the material having acquired a wear shine and a peculiar green tinge with the years. He strutted across to my table, on short stick legs hardly equal to the burden placed upon them by the roly-poly body.

I viewed his progress with an alarm triggered as much by the unaccustomed smile he bore, as by the fact that whatever business he had with me had levered him out of his comfortable chair in the main office and brought him padding across the quadrangle and down the length of the passage to the room at the end of the Infant Department block. I was taken aback. What news was so urgent that the telling of it could not wait until he sent me a summons, or so important that the conveying of it could not be entrusted to a subordinate?

That he stood to extract a measure of satisfaction from the situation was apparent.

The children had raised their heads and were watching, curious. I clapped my hands in a show of efficiency and instructed them to proceed with their sums, desperate to postpone the moment of confrontation. "You've been transferred, Miss Sloane," he said. Nothing more, nothing less. Just peered intently at me, studying my reaction.

My gaze slid off his face and became fixed on the blackboard behind his left shoulder as though, of a sudden, there existed a certain fascination in a red chalky circle, and the words "Here is a ball."

The move is to Wallawood and I'm to be there by Friday. I'll need all the warm clothes I can lay my hands on. Prevailed upon the vicar to phone his counterpart at Wallawood and between them accommodation has been arranged for me at The Chalet for tomorrow night.

From what I can gather, the place is out of the question as a permanent base—too far out of town, too *pricey* for this impecunious schoolie.

Friday, 16th June

Dark when the train drew in. Caught the only taxi, to the rambly two-storied guest-house. Walked to the school, this morning, along Main Street—a handful of ageing verandahed shops, mostly one-off with no competition.

The sign for Wallawood Primary School pointed to the river running behind those shops to the left of the road. Thought initially I'd have to swim, until I spotted the narrow footbridge. The atmosphere is crisp: I had to pull on two bulky sweaters. The Yarra here is swifter, clearer, and noisy. Upstream a diving board and a rope trailing from a peppercorn wait for summer. The wattles must be a picture when they are out.

There was no evidence of a building of any description on the far bank. Had to ask a youngster to direct me.

I followed her up the fifty-two steps cut into the hillside—yes, I counted them. Must be a perilous trek in the wet. This is the sole access to the school, and necessities such as wood for fires have to be handed up a chain of pupils standing one per step. Or so my escort informed me. Friendly child, chatty but not precocious. She was poorly clad for the chill in the air and appeared somewhat woebegone. Kathy politely ignored my gasps and wheezes, and pretended along with me that I had paused halfway up to take in the surroundings.

The rise beyond the town is Mount Little Joe, she told me. There's no Mount Big Joe. The legend goes that the son of an Italian timber worker became lost in the thick bush on the shoulder of the mountain. For years the distraught man roamed the slopes with his haunting call, "Little Joe! Little Joe!"

She related the tale with sweet sadness. Strange little thing. She didn't speak again, and when we gained the track at the top, I went on to the small wooden school painted in traditional Education Department cream-and-green, and she melted into the gathering of children lining up on the narrow strip of leveled ground beside the building.

The headmaster said that a flat area of considerable size on the crest of the hill served as the sports field, which means more climbing for Physical Education. Even the toilets—unsewered, of course—are higher than the school, a full fifteen meters farther up.

We are a staff of four, including the Head, who teaches Composite Grades 7 and 8. Some of these rural schools are still taking pupils up to fourteen years of age, because there's not a secondary school within cooee. Such big lumps they look amongst the younger ones in the playground. Several of these boys are almost men. Indeed, on completing this year, the majority of them will take up positions alongside their fathers in the saw mill

Ed Higgins, English, late thirties, paunchy, stuffy, is in charge of Grades 5 and 6. Miss McGarvie, bordering on retirement, stern-faced, gray-haired, not very communicative, is our Infant Mistress. By the process of elimination, I knew that placed me in Composite 3 and 4, long before the Head outlined my duties. I like him—slim, fine sense of humor, smiley eyes, but married, pity about that.

My stomach dropped into my desert boots on learning that no offers had been made to provide me with accommodation. I always thought that a teacher on a country posting could find a billet, if needed, with a local family. No one seemed particularly concerned about my predicament. Whereas I could scarcely see the time out until morning recess to have a quiet weep in the staff toilet at the south end of the girls' row.

Nothing but an apple for lunch; nowhere to buy food; too uptight to eat, in any case.

A knock at my door as the final bell rang. It was Higgins.

Good old, paunchy, stuffy Ed! His landlady at Wallawood House wished to know would I care to stay with her. Would I!

Thursday, 22nd June

No hope of keeping these entries up-to-date. Frantically busy. For some reason, not altogether clear to me, Miss McGarvie has been permitted to shunt a dozen of her Grade 2 into my room. Forty-six! And the regulation states a maximum of thirty pupils in a composite class. (Something to be said for Mr. Rule-bound Patterson after all.)

I am able to combine them all for Poetry and Storytime. However, the subject matter invariably proves too puerile for Grade 4, or over the heads of the littlies. When they should be writing their compositions, the Second Graders are eavesdropping on the History or Geography lessons of the upper groups: at least they are silent. Arithmetic and Spelling are bedlam. I spend my hours darting up and down the aisles correcting and controlling, then back to the blackboard demonstrating or setting new work for the smart alecks who have finished all the exercises and are pinching their neighbors or chattering to the person in the desk behind. Except Kathy. Why can't the others take a leaf out of her book? It's as if she knows instinctively when I'm at snapping point. I could love that child. Wish I could devote more time to her. She has such potential.

Wednesday, ? July

I've no idea what date it is. Only that it is a weekday. Roll on, the weekend!

It has rained incessantly for a fortnight, and snowed on the mountains. I've taken to wearing spencers. Who would believe it! There's no shortage of such antiquated lines at the General Store. Stocked up on skeins of wool, as well, and have two sweaters on the go—one for me and a matching one for Kathy. She'll be delighted. And I can cease worrying about the bones showing through those skimpy garments of hers, and the thin wrists poking out from fraying cuffs.

The Head has assigned me one of his "big boys." As a result, even when I turn up early, there's a fire roaring up the chimney. It's another of this lad's responsibilities to keep replenishing the wood supply; he's free to come into our room at will. He's part of the Italian community here, a bit on the cheeky side, with a shrewd cunning look that I mistrust. From his height and the beginnings of dark down on his upper lip, I judged him to be too old for primary school. Vittorio, the Head explained, was a protégé of his; he had already mastered his adopted tongue in the twelve months since arriving from overseas; he should be able, with the help of special tuition, to bring his other subjects up to third year high school standards by Christmas. If successful, Vittorio would live above his uncle's milkbar at River Junction, a two mile bus journey from the secondary school down the valley.

The Head took the opportunity to tease me about the number of his boys to queue outside my door for First Aid. It seems I've become unofficial medical officer. Never had he seen, he said, so many of his hefty gang fronting up for splinters to be removed.

From now on we are to ladle out hot cocoa at morning recess. That should take the edge off the bitter cold for the youngsters. If only the rain would stop. Lost my balance today as I slithered in the mud while returning from the toilet block. There'll be no using the hilltop sports ground for weeks. I don't fancy trying to shepherd forty-six would-be athletes up that slimy scarp.

Friday, 21st July

Kathy arrived drenched today. I dried her hair by the fire and brushed it out. She could be rather pretty. Why doesn't her mother take more trouble? At least see that she has a raincoat? If Kathy were mine, she'd be a different person.

Vittorio entered the classroom under a stack of red gum kindling. He left without a word, but eyed us both oddly as we stood by the hearth. What goes on in that sharp brain of his?

Monday, 24th July

The workload is proving something of a strain. Hope I don't crack up.

Small comfort back here at Wallawood House. A motley collection. With the exception of one elderly couple up from Melbourne on a holiday, all others are long-term: two fellows employed at the Post Office, a railway guard, Ed and I from the school, and a dedicated alcoholic—named, of all things, Jack Frost—with claims to having been a straight man for "Mo" at the Tivoli Theatre.

Jack Frost moans and sighs in whisky-laced dreaming, deaf to threat, deaf to entreaty, and deaf to my hammering on the flimsy fibro wall which divides my dogbox of a room from his.

Ellie, waitress-cum-housemaid, this morning emptied his liquor into the basin. Perhaps I'll sleep better tonight.

Ellie is the only outside help. The rest of the chores are carried out by the proprietors and their two daughters. The elder girl, Astrid, attractive but fat, has a crush on Ed, though I think he's too obtuse to sense it.

I kept Kathy behind after school to try on the finished woolen sweater. Her pleasure was my reward. Vittorio came in to rake the ashes and quite spoiled the moment. His face, when he straightened up, was red and distorted. He walked out muttering something like "Dyke!" What he meant, I haven't the slightest notion. The more I see of him, the less I like him.

Tuesday, 1st August
It's late, but I'm wide awake. Maybe I can organize to have a room some distance from Jack Frost.

Word has come down the bush telegraph, operating between schools along the Yarra, that the District Inspector is making his way towards us. The Head is becoming edgy. Today he hauled me over the coals because the children's exercise books were untidy.

Kathy whispered to me later that their previous teacher had made it a practice to rule up the margins and headings, overnight, in readiness for the lessons to follow. I should have noticed the deterioration in presentation—the inspector certainly will! Considering it objectively, I feel that discipline, in general, has declined since I first took charge.

For our work preparation in the evenings, Ed and I share his room—no larger than mine—it at least boasts a radiator. Besides, what with the Post Office pair playing faltering duets on the piano, and the Melbourne visitors warbling away in their quavering treble, the communal lounge is not exactly conducive to concentration.

Ed has asked me to partner him at next month's local dance. It's held in the Army Drill Hall by the river, he tells me. He also told me that he's inviting me because Astrid expects him to take her. Some compliment! Still, I might go, if only to break the monotony.

Friday, 4th August
The D.I. is due any day. The Head has requested me to re-do the friezes along the top of the other blackboards, after admiring the William Tell theme on mine. So the Infants now have the misadventures of Epaminondas, and I've rubbed off the much retraced Animals of the World of the upper school and redrawn them afresh. Kathy stayed back to pass up the colored chalks. I gave her an appreciative hug for her thoughtfulness and we walked through the town together.

Monday, 7th August

A bad day. Slipped while showering, then struck my hip on the bath tap as I struggled to my feet. Everything went black and I all but lost consciousness. Had the presence of mind to seize the cold tap and turn it on full. The shock revived me and I found myself kneeling in the bath in almost ten centimeters of water, while from the shower-rose directly above me gushed forth an icy stream onto the nape of my neck.

The door was locked. What if I had fainted? Who would have known?

On regaining my room I felt so wobbly that I decided to give school a miss. Hope Kathy won't become anxious.

The D.I. was at the school, Ed informed me at dinner, and enquired as to my whereabouts. He's calling again, especially to "crit" me, tomorrow. Now I feel worse than ever. Wish I *had* drowned.

A letter was on the hall tray for me. No signature. "Everyone is aware that you go to Ed Higgins's room every night."

Resolved to bluff it out. With much forced laughter, I handed the page around the dining table for all to read. The act misfired. Eyes avoided mine, and Ed has begged me not to prepare lessons with him again.

Who sent it? Astrid? Jack Frost? Ed?

For that matter, the traffic of guests in and out of their quarters, and along the connecting verandah, would be no secret to a person keeping vigil from the roadway below. But who would bother?

Tuesday, 8th August

Somehow I got through the day. Melted my best Dyomee bra on the iron, my thoughts on the D.I. and not the temperature setting.

Noticed two figures taking a short cut through the scrub high above the road. I think one was Kathy.

The D.I. turned out to be my former lecturer from Teachers' College, which eased the tension but left me drained nonetheless. He kept me talking long after I'd dismissed the class. Kathy was well ahead of me on the steps. She didn't hear me call. Perhaps it was because she was conversing with Vittorio.

Thursday, 10th August

Surprised Kathy and Vittorio *canoodling* by the fire when I arrived ahead of time to write up the tests on the board. The sight sickened me. Sent him packing with a warning that, if he so much as brushed against the child in the future, I would report him to the Head and he could kiss goodbye to his chance of advanced studies.

For an instant it appeared that he was about to defy me, but he sauntered insolently towards the door. As he drew level with me, he hissed, "Lesbian!"

I had a heart-to-heart talk with Her Ladyship. Think I've set her straight.

Monday, 14th August

The paper shop has lent us a window for a craft display. Kathy is inspired when it comes to plasticene models. I've ranged her pieces along the front edge. Such prominence is bound to mollify her if she's harboring a grudge after my sharpness last week.

Friday, 18th August

The Head took me aside today. I waited to hear his congratulations. Throughout the week, people have been congregating outside Smyrk's News Agency. Everybody, it seems, has at least one relative attending the school. The display has become quite an event.

He wanted to have a serious talk with me, he said. He had consulted the D.I. They both agreed I should apply for a transfer. He said he had received a letter. Something about me. About me and one of my girls.

Born in Victoria, in 1933, Margot Titcher taught primary school until her marriage. She has been writing since 1973 and her stories have been published in Australia, New Zealand and the USA. She has won several prizes in short story contests in Australia and one in New Zealand. Mrs. Titcher's interests include genealogical research and photography.

"What he had dreaded was happening."

The Sand Fox

BY GUO XUEBO

MANGOS Manha—The Demon's Desert—is what the local people called the boundless stretch of barren land in the southwest of the well-known Horqin Grassland.

In the distant past, this had been a rich, fertile land with rolling, verdant grass. The land began to show signs of sand in the Sui and Tang Dynasties over a thousand years ago. Even in the *History of the Qing Dynasty* and *Nomadic Life in Mongolia* it was recorded that the place had "good pasture, plenty of water and a lot of game" and had been the Qing Emperor Nurhachi's hunting ground. Later, people began to farm the grassland, perhaps feeling that they ought to reap such fertile land, finally bringing calamity on themselves. The sand buried under the grass was exposed and began to loosen in the sun and shift in the wind. Helped by the wind, sand from the Mongolian Desert in the west crept eastward to be cradled in the Mangos. In a mere few hundred years, forty million *mu* of fertile land became a dead, deserted world of rolling sand.

The area west of the Mangos was a barren waste, while in the east, where sand dunes rippled, desert plants like sandwort and wormwood grew sparsely. Homesteads sprawled here and there on the dunes, still farming the sand, which yielded very little. In the days of wild enthusiasm in the late fifties, an army of laborers arrived carrying a banner inscribed: "Wrest grain from the desert!" They dug three feet deep, doing devastating damage to the dunes, where vegetation was already deteriorating. They had not stayed there long before a sandstorm buried their tents, forcing them to take to their heels, yet even this did not dampen their blind enthusiasm.

The homesteads on the dunes had retreated twenty kilometers east to Green Sand Town when a forestry center was set up to tackle the sand. A man was needed to stay behind to look after the surviving desert plants.

But who would do it:

Behind a group of farmers with bowed heads, now employees of the new forestry center, a slow, hoarse voice spoke up:

"Let me."

The eyes of the bearded center chief lit up: Of course! Who would be more suitable than this ex-convict, who had been sent there from the interior? A man with no wife, no children and no belongings except two chopsticks, he had no one to worry about. The chief slapped him on the shoulder. "You're a damn good fellow. I'll wipe your slate clean for this. You're the master of the Mangos now. You belong to the desert."

He stayed there twenty years. Perhaps his life had been too unstable up till then, and he was attracted by the tranquility of the place. He often murmured softly to the yellow sand, "You are a demon. Who let you out of the bottle? How am I to get you in again? It's Heaven's punishment." He repeated it every day while putting in willow saplings beside his house and sowing rue, camel grass and other plants on the dunes to hold down the sand. Beard came sometimes and urged him, "Don't do that. It's no use. These dunes are hopeless. Sooner or later you'll have to leave here too." He protested inwardly. Leave here? Where am I to go? Can I leave the world? He went on planting. Unsure of his real name, people began to call him Old Sandy Man from his long tenure in the sand dunes. Later the story leaked out that he had been born in a village on the dunes, and that one night during a sandstorm bandits had plundered the house and killed his parents. When the house was finally buried by the shifting sand, he had joined a group of bandits to avenge his parents but had been sent to prison for it. Nobody believed that an honest and docile man like him could have been a bandit. Anyway, no one cared much about his past. All they knew about him was that he was a capable man and down to earth.

Later, Beardy brought along a woman deserted by her husband because he and his mother had condemned her for being barren. "Try to make a living together," he said. This "barren" woman bore him a daughter and died giving birth to a second child. He named their daughter Willow.

From that time on, tiny footprints appeared on the soft sand, trotting along like a lion cub beside the mother lion.

"What is that running over there, Daddy?" asked the daughter. She was always asking about the sand dunes.

"A hare. A small animal that lives in the dunes."

"Catch it, Daddy. I want it."

"No. We mustn't do that, child. We mustn't hurt a single blade or grass or insect here."

"Why?"

"Because we have so few living things here, and life depends on other life. You'll understand when you grow up."

She grew into a girl of eighteen, ruddy and well-proportioned and as pretty as a willow. In the last two years people had begun to contract land and be responsible for its output. Old Sandy and his daughter applied to contract the sand dunes the forestry center was giving up. "Do you want to live by selling sand, Old Sandy?"

"If you live on a mountain, you live off the mountain; if you live by the water, you live off the water. I live on the sand, and I'll live off the sand."

"Live off the sand? Ha ha ha!"

A rare "yellow quiet" ruled the dunes. The air seemed to stand still, as if all the wind had played itself out. The desert rested quietly like a slumbering animal. In the southeast, the sun hung on the edge of the desert behind a white pall, as yellow and lackluster as a burnt corn cake.

Sandy squinted at the weird and extraordinary sun in the southeast, shook his head and bent down to resume his examination of footprints. Beside a bush of gray wormwood, the footprints of an animal were clearly visible. He coughed again, his face red with the effort as he tried to bring up the phlegm in his throat. He panted hoarsely.

"Just gone by, my beauty, just gone by." He swung the rats in his hand excitedly.

"Dad!" his daughter called, weeding a plot of rue she had planted.

"Your droppings are green and thin. You can't have eaten any rats for days, poor thing." He was oblivious to his daughter's voice as he whispered to himself, spreading out the rats along the path of the animal.

"Look at you, Dad, all taken up with that sand fox again." She pouted as she approached. "We haven't set eyes on a man for over six months. I've almost forgotten what one looks like. Let's go to the center, Dad."

"A man? Well, you silly girl, just look at your dad if you want to know what one looks like."

"You? No, Dad, you and I don't count. Men might have sprouted wings and an extra head nowadays, for all we know." Her eyes gazed into the distant east with longing, and she sighed softly. "The dunes are stuffy and hemmed in. I'd love to go to the center and watch the people going in and out of the cinema and see a film."

"Silly girl!" Sandy shook his head helplessly and bent to his work again, unable to satisfy his daughter's longings. "The smell will lead you here, sweetie. I haven't seen you for months, old lady. Have you dropped your litter yet? I'm worried about you." After he had placed the rats on the track he squinted long at the line of footprints.

A few years before, the dunes had been plagued by rats that made holes everywhere and darted around under your feet. The stretches of carefully cultivated plants withered as their roots were eaten by the rats, which, like the desert, did their part to bring calamity to man. The old man had been mad with rage. He had laid traps, dug up rat holes and put down poison. Yet, instead of killing the rats, he had poisoned his hens. Later, he had discovered to his surprise that the rats were decreasing and disappearing. He had been bewildered. One day, when he was walking around with a gun, he had spotted animal footprints jumbled together with traces of rats. Following the footprints, he had soon discovered a roan animal under a bush, a young, limping sand fox that must have been hurt by a big animal and come to the deserted dunes to nurse its wound. When the fox yelped at him, he had instinctively raised his gun, when his heart had leapt at a new discovery. That little fox had a rat in its mouth, and there were rat legs and tails scattered outside its den. As the fact came home to him, he had slowly put down his gun and retreated. The arrival of this stranger who could tackle the rats and protect the desert plants better than he could had pleased him. His respect for an animal he had not liked up till then had risen mightily when a technician at the center had told him that a sand fox ate three thousand rats a year. He had built a den in a bush for the fox, which had made its home there. After its wound had healed, it had sometimes gone away for a few months but always returned to the place, a retreat perhaps from two-legged and four-legged hunters. It liked the dunes as well as the old man did, and between them had grown a mutual understanding that neither would hurt the other but would live peacefully together deep in the desert and keep each other company.

Now both were old. Pregnant again, the sand fox was giving birth in some secret retreat. He mustn't search for her, as a female animal was so very protective of her young. All he could do was catch rats and leave them on her track.

The old man sighed and coughed again. The hot days and cold nights of the desert hurt his windpipe and lungs and gave him bad asthma. His back and legs were failing too.

"If only that vixen could turn into a person, Dad," said his daughter melancholically. "They used to say that foxes turned into beautiful girls. Do you think they turn into young men, too?"

Sandy threw a silent glance at his daughter as the hard wrinkles on his face deepened, suddenly realizing that she had grown up. He couldn't tie her young heart down any more. He would ask Beardy to have her transferred to the center. This was what he had been dreading. He was aware that only the desert and the old vixen would stay with him all his life. Fate had brought him here, and he would never leave this demon of a place. He had an inkling that his misfortunes—his miserable life and the early death of his parents—had something to do with this demon. He had manipulated it. For half a lifetime he had tried to make a living on both sides of the Great Wall, and ending up in this place was the work of this demon, too. He had no fear, but rather icy hatred. He looked up again at the strange sun. The white sand clouds beneath it were thickening, moving slowly and heavily. The old man pommeled his back and mumbled, "Who let you out of the bottle, demon? Are you going wild again?"

"Hey! Sandy!"

Two men on horseback called outside his home. A man took off his hat and waved at them.

"Ah! Someone has come, Dad! We have visitors!" his daughter cried with joy.

"Yes. Who are they?" The old man rubbed his eyes and looked hard. "Beardy? Who's with him?"

"Little Yang, the secretary. Hurry up, Dad. We mustn't keep them waiting." She dragged him in the direction of their home.

"How have you been getting along, old chap?" The center chief still had a bushy beard and was just as straightforward as ever.

"So so."

"Only so so? With all the land you've contracted and all you've grown? Why, the seeds alone will fetch five yuan sixty a kilo. You'll be rolling in money." He spoke as if the land would yield gold and crops shoot up like bamboo after rain. Beardy joked happily and slapped the old man on the shoulder.

Sandy laughed. He was fond of the man, although aware that he had drawn twenty years' pay as the head of the forestry center for doing less in the way of sand prevention and afforestation than in that of making himself a name for drinking and hunting. "What brings you here, boss?"

"Well, I'm off to be advisor to the county forestry bureau. I've come to pay you and the dunes a visit before I go," said Beardy with feeling. "I'm sorry to have left you here in the dunes for all of twenty years. How about having you transferred to the center before I leave for good?"

"Oh, no, I like it here. I don't want to leave. This is home to me, ha, ha!"

"You're a stubborn old man. I want to do something for you before I leave. You may make one request."

"Well—I do have a small request." The old man threw a glance at his daughter, then hesitated. "Well, no, I suppose I don't. Not really."

The daughter chimed in: "Ask the visitors in, Dad. What are you standing there for? I'll make you something to eat." She was buoyant, stealing glances at the fair-complexioned young secretary.

"Ah, yes, come inside. I have some good wine, too." Perking up, the old man briskly invited the visitors in.

"There's no rush. We have all day." Beardy looked at the sky and then around at the dunes. "We'll just take a turn round the dunes and see your plants."

"Well—" Sandy looked at him, pondering what he had said. His heart had missed a beat at that "just take a turn"—and his glance fell on Beardy's shotgun. The secretary had a gun, too. "Okay, you can look around. But why are you carrying guns?"

"Just a precaution. What if we should come across some wolf in the dunes?" Beardy joked.

"Hm." Sandy thought for a while. "How about this, boss?" He blurted out, "Don't bother walking round. Just shoot at my chickens. I don't fancy keeping them and I don't know what to do with them."

Beardy was stunned. Then he shook his head and laughed. "You're a strange old man. I'm telling you, we'll just take a turn."

He could say nothing, despite his apprehensions. He spoke gruffly to his daughter: "Take them around the dunes, child."

"No, no, there's no need. We're on horseback. She can't keep up with us."

"She can take the donkey. We have a donkey. It's only right for her to show the boss around." The old man insisted stubbornly that his daughter should go with them on the donkey, and she seemed happy to do so.

Beardy had to comply with his host's wishes.

So the three of them, two on horseback, one on a donkey, set out along a twisting path into the dunes.

Full of misgivings, the old man gazed after the departing party and then moved his stiff legs towards the chickens in his yard. Here in the desert, he usually let them roam the dunes, so they were quite wild. He chased them and couldn't catch a feather. Panting and angry, he collected the eggs, went in for a handful of rice and called them. The chickens quickly followed him in. He closed the door behind them.

The room was instantly in a commotion as the chickens cackled and fluttered among the pots and rice bowls.

A shot rang out from way down the dunes as the old man was happily slaughtering his chickens. He did it in a strange way, breaking the chicken's spine first, twisting its head round to tuck under a wing, then dashing it to the ground so that its legs stretched and went stiff. In this way he killed six, one for each person to eat and two for the men to take away. He did not grudge them, for chickens, growing mainly on their own in the dunes, were nothing precious. The sound of the gunshot stunned him. He gaped and dashed outside, cocking his ear towards the dunes, but they had fallen silent again.

"Perhaps it went off accidentally, or they were shooting for fun," he consoled himself. He returned indoors, where the six plucked chickens lay in a row on the chopping board waiting to be cooked.

"Bang! Bang!" More shots rang out.

Jumping up as if scalded, he dashed out and looked towards the dunes, his heart contracting. What he had dreaded was happening. They were hunting.

He knew on his finger tips how many hares and pheasants there were in the dunes. After he had contracted and planted the dunes, animals and birds had begun to appear in the last few years. It was now breeding time. It wouldn't do to slaughter them like this. He could have kicked himself.

The thought of the fox made him shudder. She had cubs. Let her stay clear of them. His anxiety carried him flying towards the dunes. But where were they? His chest heaved as he panted along. He stopped to take a breath and looked around at the world he was so familiar with. He knew every mound, every plant and that everything was governed by heat and drought, evaporation being twenty times precipitation. The plants, in order to survive, grew abnormally. Tamarisks cut down the size of their leaves to decrease evaporation. The leaves of others had entirely degenerated, so that photosynthesis was carried out by their trunks and branches. Some had turned gray to reflect and survive in the strong light and oppressive ultraviolet rays. To survive in the adverse environment, all lives in the desert struggled every moment against death. He admired the plants and animals in the desert and looked upon them as his models and companions, heroes defying the demon. To fight the demon desert, men, animals and plants had formed a harmonious, natural liaison.

He pulled himself together and proceeded.

A rider approached. It was his daughter. He looked silently at her face, from which all signs of joy were gone. Head bowed, she dared not meet her father's eyes.

"They are hunting."

He gazed at her silently.

"They're shooting our hares and pheasants."

The old man's gaze was still fixed on his daughter's exhausted face.

"And they're good shots too, damn them. Is everyone outside these dunes as wicked?"

Only then did he speak, coldly. "Didn't I send you just to show them around?"

"I tried to stop them. I shouted. I tried to take their guns," she quickly explained. "Beardy ignored me. Little Yang said, "Hares and pheasants are wild. They're not your old man's chickens and rabbits. You've contracted the dunes, not the hares and pheasants.'"

The old man's jaw dropped.

"Did they get...a lot?" he muttered after a time.

"Three pheasants, five hares, and..."

"And what? Out with it."

"The fox."

"What about her?"

"They found her den and they're chasing her."

"Why the hell did you come back then, you idiot? Why didn't you stop them and save her?" The enraged old man raised a fist. Veins throbbed on his forehead, and blood rushed to his face.

"They followed her into the desert; my donkey couldn't keep up." She stood before her father, braving his wrath with a sad smile at the corners of her mouth. "She was brave. She ran out of her den with two cubs in her mouth and one on her back straight into the desert."

"The desert?" His fist dropped, his sunken cheeks twitched, and his eyes turned to the deep desert in the west. "They've gone into the desert?"

A wind rose in the southeast, all the plants on the dunes swayed, and the white sand clouds that had gathered under the sun moved into the Manogs. A bad storm was on its way.

"Dad." She swept a scared glance at the southeast where she could see nothing now except a long, hazy wave rolling rapidly nearer. "Let's hurry home, Dad. The well isn't covered."

Still he stood and looked towards the west. "The desert. They went into the desert." She dragged him after her as she ran towards home. The ominous wave, bowling along just above the ground, caught up with them as they reached home. The sand rustled in the wind, which carried fallen leaves and broken grasses up to the darkening sky. The sun shielded by a wall of yellow sand, hung listlessly over the desert like a yellow-painted balloon, devoid of its usual menace.

But the wind was scorching, licking at their backs through their clothing as it rolled in from the desert. Sand made its way into their ears and mouths and eyes. As the wind reached a climax, it shook the desert.

"The wicked sandstorm! The cursed demon!" She spat as she ran to cover the well, shoo in the chickens and close the door and windows.

His brows tightly knit, the old man gazed speechlessly towards the west.

"Dad?"

"They won't get in from the desert in a storm as bad as this."

"It serves them right."

"It'll cover every footprint and landmark." The old man's face hardened. "They'll be lost out there."

"Forget about them. We didn't ask them to go."

"Listen, child. Fill a bucket with water and pack some rations."

"Dad?"

"Get moving."

"No, Dad. You're too weak. You're ill."

Unheeding, he went to the outer room, filled a bucket and put all their corn buns and parched flour into a bag. Then he fetched some clothing from the inner room and began to tie up his waist and trouser-legs.

"You mustn't go, Dad, please," she begged, throwing herself at his feet and hugging his legs.

"They will die with no water or food, child. The demon is after them. And the fox, too."

"But you're not well. You won't be able to breathe in the storm. You'll kill yourself instead of saving them."

"I can stick it out. This will keep my asthma under control." He pulled out a bottle of wine and took a swig.

"No. Let me go. You stay here, Dad. Let me go."

"You'll get lost out there. You don't know it well enough. I know this demon. I can find them. Get up, child, and let me set out. Now." An unswerving, steely resolution showed on the old man's solemn face.

"No. I won't let you go. No!" She clutched his legs tighter.

He shoved her away and plunged into the raging sandstorm carrying the water, rations and clothes.

"Dad!"

She scrambled to her feet, took her father's stick from behind the door and plunged into the storm, too, while the door slapped and banged behind her.

Father and daughter trudged along in the blazing desert.

For a day and a night they found nothing. The storm never let up, continuing to swallow everything with smothering force. The willow leaves shriveled, drooping like hanging rags. Dark sand gathered like black flour under the sandwort bushes. All the leaves of the plants that had grown sparsely and with difficulty in the desert withered and became so dry that they crumbled between one's fingers, and the wind stripped the leaves off their branches in no time. It was a cruel world.

Sandy trudged like an old camel. He shielded his eyes with his left hand and held his stick in his right, stopping every few steps to cough. Sometimes, when the wind was too strong for him to breathe, his face turned purple as he fought for breath, and he would turn around and take a sip of his wine. His daughter, who tagged behind him with the bucket of water and the rations, sometimes helped him to pull his feet out of the soft sand.

When the wind let up in the afternoon of the second day, the desert plunged suddenly into silence. The hopping, moving, wild sands were now as docile and quiet as a child who has misbehaved and is now waiting for punishment. The demon was tired out after a night and two days' wildness.

The old man's eyes searched the rolling, yellow sand that stretched all around him endlessly, monotonously and dizzyingly. Was all the world made up of sand? You couldn't see a thread of green or hear a single chirp of insect or bird. At times like this, one might be consoled even by the buzzing of a fly; the existence of precious life would drive away the dreadful shadow that gripped one's heart. But no. There was no sign of life except one's own scorching breath. The frightened daughter gripped her father's clothes. The old man's lips were cracked and bleeding, but he shook his head when she handed him the water bottle. They had used up a lot of water without finding the two men. Who knew how long they would have to stay in the desert?

Beneath a sloping sand bank, she saw a dark spot and ran to it. It was the tip of a saddle protruding from beneath a sand drift. Unable to pull it out, she dug away the sand and was alarmed to find a dead horse beneath the saddle. She screamed.

"Come here, Dad."

The old man realized that the horse must have been frightened, left its rider in the storm and been buried by the sand.

"Where's the rider?" asked the daughter.

The old man silently looked around at the sand-hills.

"How did you know they came this way, Dad?"

"I guessed it. The fact that the fox escaped into the desert with her cubs was proof that she had a den here. But where would she dig a hole in the drifting sand? Then I remembered that there was a ruined city here that I had taken some archaeologists to a few years back. She could only have made a hole here. So I headed straight for this place."

"But where is the ruined city? I can't see it."

"The storm has changed the lay of the land. We'll walk on and see."

They proceeded.

By dusk they finally found the two men on top of a high dune. Half of Beardy's body was buried, his thick bushy beard filled with sand. His eyes closed tight, his head turned to one side, he must have stuck out his tongue and licked the sand, for his tongue was sand-covered. The secretary was crouched face down as if fallen into a long-awaiting dream. His hand clutched at his chest, which must have been burning inside him.

Sandy licked his dry lips and heaved a long sigh.

"Look what you get, all for a sand fox. At least you've chosen a good spot. If you'd collapsed beneath the slope you'd have ended up like your horse."

The old man flung his stick away, crouched down and with his daughter helped the two men up. He carefully gave them water, and they gradually came to. Then he fed them parched flour mixed with water.

They revived.

"Oh, it's you, old fellow. Thank you." Beardy smiled wryly.

The secretary showed his sincere gratitude, too.

What's the use of your gratitude? the old man thought as he rose silently and tossed them the clothes he had brought. "Put them on. It's freezing at night. You hunters will be frostbitten."

He moved away to look around. The sun had set. He saw

nothing in the dusk. Sure enough, the sand emitted a cold which floated up, spread and chilled the air. The old man coughed painfully while his daughter pounded his back gently. Beardy and the secretary looked at him.

"Where is the fox you were after?" the old man suddenly demanded.

The two men looked at each other speechlessly.

"Well, where is it?" the old man boomed. They jumped as he looked at them with eyes like cold knives.

"We didn't get it. Honestly. It ran faster than a horse in the desert. And then we got lost in the storm," Beardy explained awkwardly.

The old man turned away, not wanting to look at their faces any longer. He moved a few steps further and gazed for a long time into the hazy, mysterious distance, his swarthy face expressionless.

"Let's go home, Dad. It's scary here." She walked up and touched his elbow softly. He nodded, took the bucket, filled his water bottle and returned the bucket to her, saying, "You get them out of the desert. Go straight east to where the moon rises. You'll be out by dawn."

"What about you, Dad?" Her heart pounded with fear.

"I'll look for her. She has cubs and no water. They'll die of thirst." He never took his eyes off the gloomy desert.

She shuddered silently. After a long pause she asked, "Is the ruined city very far?"

"I don't know. Probably not. Maybe just ahead."

"Well then, Sandy, after that fox?" said Beardy, picking up bits and pieces of their conversation. "Good for you! The damned beast almost killed us." He patted his gun, which he still had. The secretary had lost his.

The old man shook his head with a wry smile. He didn't want to explain anything at a time like this. Would Beardy, who had always enjoyed hunting, understand his feelings for the fox? He turned to his daughter. "Off you go now. When you pass that dead horse, be sure to cut a large chunk of meat. Your rations won't last long."

She nodded quietly, looking tearfully at him. She bit hard at a corner of her scarf to keep from breaking down. She knew he would never turn back once the decision was made, which made her put all the blame on the two men before her. They had come to this place and disturbed its quiet, its peace and its ecological balance and brought the few lives in the desert to the brink of death.

"Don't go, sir. You can't just leave us to her!" said the wretched young secretary.

"Hah! I can guarantee your lives, you coward," shouted the hurt girl at the man from the envied center. She hardened instantly and told her father, "Off you go, Dad. I'll get them out of this place and then come back for you."

"Trust her. She's reliable," the old man said calmly. She picked up his stick for him and took off her coat to wrap around his shoulders.

The desert at night was like a black sea stretching out silently before them, profound, mysterious and unfathomable, as if waiting to swallow all life that dared to challenge it.

Sandy straightened up and made his way into this black sea. "I'll be back for you, Dad. Take care." The daughter followed him a few steps, her eyes moist. He soon disappeared into the darkness of the sandy sea. From time to time a few laborious coughs could be heard in the distance.

Willow was startled from her sleep by a shout. The night before, when she had taken the two men to the dead horse, they had been so tired out they had had to make camp in the open.

"What's that? Look!" shouted Beardy.

She looked. Forty meters to the east, on a sand hill, stood the fox, her fur like a flickering ball of fire, extremely attractive in the morning rays as she suckled a cub, her maternal posture revealing no inclination to interrupt the feeding and run for her life.

"That damned beast! So it's here." The sight of the fox worked Beardy up so much that he grabbed his gun.

The fox must have been attracted by the smell of the dead horse. Her hunger had led her here. Where were her other two cubs? The one with her must be the weakest, which often gets the most protection, with animals as with human beings. The fox gazed at the group of three, opening her mouth and licking her dry lips.

Then unexpectedly she stood up her hind legs, showing her beautiful white chest, and waved her forelegs at the people; perhaps this was how foxes greeted. The cub rose between her two legs along with its mother and held on to the nipple, hanging there like a gourd. Then the fox seemed to sense the danger. But instead of running away, she looked with pleading, pitiful red eyes at the human beings who were masters of the world.

The girl was stunned by what she saw.

"Its fur is damn pretty. I've never got such a beautiful fox in all my life. I haven't suffered for nothing." Beardy was flustered with excitement.

He took aim with a quivering finger.

"Don't shoot. Please. You mustn't!" Startled, Willow threw herself madly at Beardy.

Too late.

A sharp shot shook the quiet morning of the desert. Its terrible echo reverberated there for a long time.

The fox fell, blood gushing from where the bullet had pierced her chest and seeping into the loose sand, which instantly turned dark brown. Her eyes were still open, gazing at the blue sky with helpless sadness, while two tears stood at the corners of her eyes. The poor cub still clutched at her teat, sucking greedily at the blood-stained nipple that yielded no milk.

Beardy was dazed and frightened. "Heaven," he said, putting his head in his hands. "What have I done?"

He flopped down on the sand, looking first at the dead fox and her wailing cub and then at the gun in his listless hand. All his life he had thought hunting justified, but today he was bewildered, wondering if he had done right. He felt the desert expanding, squeezing and pressing down on him. Men were so insignificant here, so lonely and helpless.

A man came walking towards them over the desert. He was coughing as he walked, and in a single night he had become much older: sand filled the wrinkles on his face; he had lost his hat and his gray hair was all disheveled; his bent body seemed about to fall with the next gust of wind. But he proceeded with firm steps, following the track of the fox. Suddenly he stopped and stood, not believing what he saw, rooted to the ground, rubbing his old eyes with his sleeves. After a while, he advanced slowly, knelt down beside the fox and caressed her head with shuddering hands. With trembling fingers he closed her tearful eyes while two bitter tears rolled from his own eyes. He knelt there quietly, his head bowed. Remembering something, he fumbled in his bag and produced two fox cubs, which he placed beside the one on the sand, then began to give the three motherless cubs water.

None of them drank. All crawled laboriously towards their mother, the weakest falling flat in the struggle, unable to right itself for a long time. Each took a blood-stained nipple.

Sandy's face twitched. He rose abruptly and went towards Beardy, who stood there woodenly awaiting punishment. Sandy halted in front of him with a stern face and cold, boring eyes, then grabbed Beardy's gun, broke it on his knee and tossed it away, howling like a beast, "Damn you, you desert demon! It's all your fault. I hate you. Who let you out of the bottle? Who was it?"

His hoarse voice bellowed over the quiet, boundless desert, which felt nothing and breathed death. To the desert, men were insignificant.

"I'm scared, Dad." Willow came up and took his arm. "Let's go home. I miss it. That's the best place, at home on our sand dunes. I'll never leave them." She picked up the three cubs and clutched the warm little lives close to her body.

They started out eastwards, to their green home, leaving firm footprints in the barren waste. The wind rose again, chasing after them and covering up their footprints, pushing them along, trying to swallow and overtake them as it swooped into the east.

Born in 1950, in Inner Mongolia, Guo Xuebo graduated from the Department of Dramatic Literature of the Central Academy of Drama in 1980. His first short story was published in 1975. He has published short stories, a novella and a novel. He is the literary editor at the Countryside Reader Publishing House. Yu Fanqin translated this story.

"That was just the problem."

The Princess

BY IRENA IOANNIDOU ADAMIDOU

"YOU know, I've got a cousin at Polis," said my friend, as the car left Paphos behind.

"A first cousin?"

"Second."

"Fine! Let's go and see her. Do you know where she lives?"

"No. I've never been here before. And I haven't seen her for years, not since the time she came to our house with her mother. I was a little girl. I'm sure she wouldn't recognize me now."

"I don't suppose it would be difficult to find her. In villages everyone knows each other."

"That's true. That family especially must be well known. It was the leading one in Polis. And their house was one of the oldest and finest."

"Oh-ho! An important person, then, your cousin!" I laughed.

My friend nodded her head sadly.

"Yes, before...She was really the richest and the most beautiful girl in the district. 'The Princess!' That's what they called her. I remember her when she came to our house. I stood in open-mouthed astonishment. My goodness, how beautiful she was! She wore a dress of silk and some old jewelry worth a fortune. She was absolutely dazzling! Now, of course, she must have changed. So many years have gone by."

"Didn't she get married?"

"She did but..."

I waited for her to finish her sentence. But she left it there and turned to look out of the window.

"What happened? Did her husband die?"

"No, no! Just that she married late and the man turned out to be the wrong one."

"Why did she marry late? From what you tell me she must have been much sought after."

"That was just the problem. Her mother was to blame. She thought that anyone who asked for her daughter's hand was interested only in her money and so she rejected the suitors one after another."

"And what did the girl say?"

"Nothing. She was a quiet type without a will of her own. She let her mother handle everything, even her own life."

"What about her father?"

"He died when she was only a few months old."

"Didn't she study anything?"

"No. I'm not even sure if she completed her secondary education."

"What a shame! With so much money she could have studied something. And she would have been independent as well."

"Of course, she could have! But she didn't. Her mother wouldn't let her. You know the village mentality: 'There is no need for rich girls to study.' "

"It's a crime!"

"I agree. But what's to be done? When people have ideas like that, they don't change them easily."

"How old was your cousin when she got married?"

"About forty."

"And her husband?"

"I heard that he is at least fifteen years younger."

"Oh! Then you're right when you say that they are not suited."

"I didn't say it for that. He is a gambler, her social inferior and he is squandering her fortune."

"How terrible! How did her mother accept such a son-in-law when so many others had not pleased her?"

"What was she to do? When she saw the years slipping by and her daughter in danger of being left on the shelf, she was forced to compromise. When you're forty, you see, you don't choose. You take what you can get."

We spoke no more about her cousin until we reached Polis. The man who was to show us the sights happened to be her neighbor and said that if we wanted, he could take us to her mansion. That's just how he put it: "to her mansion."

From the outside it really looked a gracious old house.

As soon as we entered, my first thought was that Attila had been through but had been generous enough to allow the owners to stay in their house and even to keep a few essentials: four chairs, a table leaning against one wall and a refrigerator on another.

The woman who opened the door seemed about sixty. In vain I tried to find on her face just a trace of that former beauty which my friend had once so admired. Yet something in her expression, in her toothless mouth, in her manners, revealed her background which, of course, nothing could destroy. However, it sometimes can be so well masked by suffering, that you must search to discover it—as often happens in the case of valuable works of art which have been painted over.

I remained standing by the door, like a statue, while my friend tried to explain to her cousin who she was. When the woman finally understood, she embraced her and burst into tears. Then she began asking about their other relatives who lived in Nicosia and whom she had not seen for many years. Most of them were dead, but she took the sad news dry eyed and almost indifferently. She only said, on hearing of each death, "Really? The poor soul!"

She hesitated a little before asking us to sit down. She quickly glanced at the chairs. I didn't immediately realize that she was calculating if there were enough of them for us. Then she let out a small sigh of relief. She even tried to smile at us.

"Sit down!"

She brought us some coffee and cake. Then her neighbor, who was accompanying us, asked her to show us the house.

"They must see the view from upstairs. It's really unique!"

"With pleasure! Come!"

She led the way up the wooden staircase, to the first floor. There was a landing and rooms to the right and left, half empty, like those downstairs, a double bed in one, a table and sideboard in another, with just a few photographs for ornaments, all of the same fat, moustached man. In the corner, over a chair, was a glass case with two wedding wreaths in it. It reminded me of a tiny coffin.

I saw my friend look at the ceiling and then sadly shake her head. She had done it several times since we had arrived and I wondered why. Not why she shook her head—that I understood— but why she looked at the ceiling in every room we entered.

Her cousin stepped up onto a chair and unbolted the door of the balcony. The neighbor, however, had to pull very hard before it opened, an indication that it had remained shut for a long time.

We stepped out onto the balcony. The view from there was really magnificent, with the mountains on one side and the plain on the other. We stood and marveled at it. Our hostess was beside us, ecstatic, as if she, too, were seeing it for the first time.

"What a lovely house you have," I told her, as we went down. "Solidly built and spacious. A real palace!"

Her expression did not change. "Yes, it's all right," she said indifferently.

"And what a fine marble floor! It's not easy to find one like that nowadays."

"Yes, it's all right," she repeated with the same indifference.

As she said good-bye to us at the door, her eyes filled with tears again.

"Please, come again," she said to my friend.

"And you must come to see us in Nicosia."

The woman smiled with bitter irony. "I?" Then she added unexpectedly: "I'm very sorry about the death of our relatives."

"What can we do!"

"That's it. We can't do anything."

She shook her head fatalistically for a few seconds. My friend embraced her, kissed her.

"Bye-bye. I'm so pleased to have seen you."

"Me, too. Have a good journey!"

As we drove off, I turned and saw her still standing on the doorstep, watching us.

"Poor thing," I whispered. "You saw how moved she was when she realized who you were?"

"I think she was more upset by my seeing her in such a terrible state," my friend said. "Those tears were just for herself."

"That's true," said the man who was accompanying us. "If only you knew what she was like a few years ago! A real princess! She was so charming and dignified! I can't find the words to describe her."

"How old is she now?" I asked.

"Not more than forty-seven or forty-eight."

I gasped. "I thought she was about sixty!"

"That's what everybody thinks. She ages deeply each day. You'll have realized, of course, that she suffers with her nerves."

"Yes, I suspected something. But why? Does her husband treat her badly?"

"He doesn't beat her, if that's what you mean. Why should he, anyhow? He takes from her whatever he wants without any resistance on her part. Didn't you see? He's literally ruined her!"

"I've certainly never seen such a bare house," my friend said. "And to think that her silver and jewelry were a legend in our family!"

"Now, she has nothing. He hasn't left her even a spoon! He's sold everything."

"Even her old lamps! A friend of mine, who writes about these things, told me that he hadn't found finer ones in any of the other villages he had visited."

I turned and looked at her. "That's why you kept looking at the ceiling? I was puzzled..."

"Yes, that's why. But you saw that in all the rooms there was just a flex with a naked bulb at the end."

"Truly, you can't imagine what was in there before," said our companion. Your friend was absolutely right. I haven't seen finer lamps either. But her husband sold those, too. And the old chests. Everything! Absolutely everything, I tell you! A few months ago he took her last piece of jewelry, a thick gold chain, an heirloom from goodness knows how many generations back. He took it off her just like that, while she was wearing it."

"How terrible," I whispered in horror. "Real robbery!"

"That's right! You should have seen how she behaved every time he took something from her to sell. It was as if they were killing her child. She ran out into the streets crying, beating her breast and pulling her hair. In the end she finished up in this terrible state, half crazy."

"She ought to have divorced him straight away!" I shouted angrily.

The man gave a sad smile. "Divorce him! She would never have had the courage. And you know the way people think in villages..."

"At least she should have called the police, to stop him from taking her things."

"That would have required even greater courage. The shame...you see..."

"But doesn't this woman have anyone at all to help her? That mother who wrecked her life is dead?"

"Yes. She died a few years ago."

"And now she is all alone in the world, at the mercy of that brigand?"

"That, in fact, is the position. She has some relatives left, but they don't bother about her at all. They don't want to get involved, though I believe they should. After all, it's a question of their own self-respect. Especially now that fellow has got his eye on her property as well."

"Don't tell me he would even sell her house!"

"He wants to, but it's the only time she has stood up to him. So far he has sold the house next door and some fields. But it seems that he is having difficulty in getting her to sign for this one, her family house."

"Well done! She mustn't sign!"

"That's what we say. But how long will she hold out? I'm afraid that she will give in eventually, because he is threatening to leave her if she doesn't agree."

"Let him leave her a hundred times! It's obvious that sooner or later he will, just as soon as he has spent her last penny."

"But as long as she can keep him satisfied, she has hope, the poor thing. As we said, village mentality is different. It's considered a great disgrace for your husband to leave you."

"If that mother of hers had allowed her to study, everything would have been different now," my friend said softly.

I couldn't have agreed more with her. I looked at her. She hadn't spoken for a long time. I saw bitterness in her face as she gazed out of the car window. I regretted having talked so much about her cousin and quickly changed the subject.

"Well, then, shall we go to the baths of Aphrodite?"

"As you wish," answered our companion. "I'm at your disposal."

"Let's go," said my friend. "I've never seen them."

The car headed for the coast.

For the rest of the day we spoke no more about her cousin, who once had been the "Princess" of Polis. I felt, however, that both of us had her constantly in our thoughts.

Born in Cyprus, Irene Ioannidou Adamidou started writing at 16 years of age. To date 14 of her books have been published in Athens and Nicosia. She has also written 30 plays for radio, television or stage, and many of these have been successfully produced in Cyprus and Greece. Since 1962 she has been associated with the Cyprus Broadcasting Corporation as writer and translator; she translates from French, English, Italian, Spanish and German. She is a member of the Cyprus PEN Committee for Public Relations. This story was translated by Maria Dimitriou

"My grandparents, as I was to discover,
were not my *real* grandparents."

Odessa

BY ALEX AUSWAKS

MY grandmother came from Odessa.

Russians refer to their country as "rodina," the motherland. In English it sounds dreadful and few Englishmen would raise their glasses and say, "To the motherland."

But Russians do toast their "rodina." In Russian it sounds right, produces the necessary emotional impact.

To people from the City of Odessa, the "rodina" can mean only one place. Ask them where they come from and they say, always with tremendous pride in their voice, "My 'rodina' is Odessa!"

I had no such interesting or emotive place to come from, being born and raised in a dull and dreary port called Tientsin on the North China coast. It is the port for Peking in particular and North China in general. Tientsin means "The Gates of Heaven" and as far as we were concerned, it was about as misnamed as Greenland, which Eric the Red called it, hoping it would make people go there. "If heaven is like this," we used to say, "there is a good case for sin. Who wants to be bored for all eternity?"

For those of us who were born in Tientsin, not only was it

boring, we also had no identity. We knew we did not belong. The North Chinese are a tolerant and hospitable people, but we were exiles. Other people we met were born in exciting places, like London or New York, Paris or Brussels. But we only came from Tientsin. What answer could one give to a stranger? If only one could say, "I am from...," from anywhere else on earth. My mother and father never spoke very much of their origins, but at least my grandparents came from somewhere special. One day, when I grow up, I used to say, I shall go to Odessa.

My grandparents, as I was to discover, were not my *real* grandparents. Their only son, Sasha, had been my mother's first husband, but he had died of tuberculosis. From that marriage my mother had a son, my half-brother. After her first husband died, she married my father, whom she met in Tientsin, where I was born, and here I am. But I wasn't to know anything about the circumstances till much, much later.

We all lived in a huge block of flats. My father and mother, my half-brother and I were in an apartment on the second floor. My grandparents were on the first.

My earliest memories are of the Second World War.

My brother was already a teen-ager. His parents bored him, his grandparents more so. And so, in the evenings while my father gambled, my mother busied herself round the house and my half-brother pursued his teen-age interests, it was usually I who was dispatched to visit the old people and keep them company. We became very close. I discovered much later that all the affectionate nicknames they bestowed on me during those evenings, they had first used on their little boy in Odessa.

Grandmother had no hobbies or special interests. She never took any interest in politics or the war. My grandfather, however, although he, too, was illiterate, had got hold of an old school atlas, and with the help of what little reading I was able to accomplish, kept account of the progress of various armies.

And so I remember my grandmother's interest in the war awakening as the Germans surrounded her "rodina"—Odessa.

Until wasted by disease, she was physically a large woman, usually dressed in velvet, with lace at her collar and wrists. She wore lots of jewelry, real jewelry, never took her rings off, even when she cooked and baked. She claimed that certain diamonds had magic properties and enhanced cooking. She walked and spoke with tremendous confidence. She was quite a grand old dame.

When the German iron ring closed in on Odessa in the summer and autumn of 1941, she grew quieter, more subdued. Previously, she had never been still. There was always something to supervise or to do herself, people to visit, friends to entertain. Now she sat and stared into the distance, as if she could see and hear the sound of gunfire, and then she would shudder in the stillness of her room.

As far as she knew, she had no family left in Odessa. It was Odessa itself that was her mother and father, her brother and her sister.

The Jewish New Year comes in the autumn, and unlike the international New Year, it is not a cheerful festival. Tradition has it that on the New Year, all one's deeds during the past year are examined and a sentence is provisionally handed down. From the New Year to the Day of Atonement there are ten days. These ten days are one's last opportunity to make good. Bitter enemies smile at each other benignly. Debts are paid off, borrowed goods returned. Apologies are proffered and readily accepted during that time.

The New Year, the ten intermediate days and the Day of Atonement were particularly poignant in my grandparents' home just before Odessa fell. The Day of Atonement passed in fasting. Most Jews breathe a sigh of relief when it is over. But Grandmother grew completely still. She didn't go back to telling Mother how to run her household.

Grandmother ignored the fall of Odessa when it was broadcast on German radio. Grandmother was no Communist. She held no brief for Russians. Her childhood had coincided with the Kishinev pogrom. But she waited until Moscow radio broadcast the news that Odessa had fallen.

Then Grandmother declared "shiva." For seven days and seven nights she sat on a low stool with the Book of Job open before her. Neighbors slipped in to prepare the meal of lamentation. My mother, however, saw herself as a modern woman beyond such superstitions and would have nothing to do with all this nonsense.

My grandfather arranged for ten adult males to be present for the appropriate services to be performed. Since I was under thirteen, I was not considered a fully-fledged male. My brother, who was over thirteen, pleaded that he was busy. Father, who had no "rodina" to call his own and was equally biased against all races, creeds, nationalities and religions, came thrice daily, said all the right things and avoided saying the wrong ones. The correct etiquette is laid down by Maimonides, who said we must not say to a mourner, "What can you do?" or "That's life for you!" or "You're not the only one to suffer!" Father said none of these things, although Mother said them all under her breath.

For seven days and seven nights, while Grandfather was banned to the spare bedroom (no conjugal activity during *shiva*), my grandmother observed the rules of confined mourning with the utmost strictness.

A few ultra-orthodox Jews muttered that this sort of mourning was only to be observed for members of one's family. Did she actually have her family in Odessa? they asked. Had she been informed they were dead? Some said that the ultra-orthodox had even reported to the rabbi that whereas one day had been decreed to commemorate the fall of the Temple, here was a member of his congregation observing solemn mourning in its fullest ritual for some port on the Black Sea.

It was said that the rabbi heard the ultra-orthodox out and shook his head. Well he might! Jews from Odessa do not interpret the law to suit themselves. They make their own laws.

At the end of the period of mourning, Grandfather was restored to his rightful place in her bed. Coverings were removed from all mirrors. Grandmother gave away to charity the dresses which had been ceremoniously rent three inches with my grandfather's razor. But she was a different grandmother. She no longer laid down the law to one and all. Servants bullied her. She became absent-minded. She would sit for hours with curtains drawn. Her face began to lose its healthy, vibrant look. The tuberculosis, which eventually carried her away, must have started then. She became impatient with talk of the war, as if she were waiting for the one piece of news that mattered.

Like so many others all over the world, we hoped and prayed for the tide of war to turn.

In 1944 it was the turn of the Red Army to approach Odessa.

The Jewish festival of Passover celebrates the liberation of Jews from the aegis of Egyptian pharaohs. It is a happy holiday. It also marks the start of spring. Even Mother used to buy us boys new suits and order new curtains for Passover.

The Jews of Odessa are truly religious. They are always holding dialogues with God. They now declared they were in a position to forgive God much. He had taken Odessa away following the Day of Atonement, but in His infinite mercy looked as if He were about to return it for Passover.

As for Grandmother, it wasn't just new curtains. The whole apartment was redecorated. Every vase was filled with flowers. Grandfather laid up cases of the best wines. Bottles of vodka were uncorked, stuffed with orange and lemon peel, and sealed up again to give their contents added strength.

Jewish lent begins after the second day of Passover, but Grandmother unilaterally announced its lifting together with the special dietary regulations of Passover itself.

Celebrations began when Moscow radio formally announced that Odessa was free of fascist invaders. Every cakeshop in town was cleared by Grandfather that day. In accordance with custom, when one celebrates a happy event, food and cakes are sent to the local old people's home, the orphanage and hospital. But there was more than enough for everyone else. "I want the whole world to celebrate," said Grandmother. And just about the whole world piled into her apartment.

Grandfather was gloriously drunk and poured drinks for everyone as if he possessed a bottomless well full of wines and spirits. Grandmother pressed food and cake on an endless stream of guests.

Late in the day Grandmother's doctor arrived. Dr. Gurevitch was a huge man, with a large bald head and a tiny moustache on his broad face. He had been listening to the radio all day, while the feasting had been in progress. He brought more up-to-date news.

During the Second World War, as the Red Army first retreated and then advanced, many individual acts of heroism were carried out by soldiers defending and later liberating the very towns and villages in which they had been born and raised. In fact, there was a war-time expression: "Who's first?" This referred to the soldier who was first over the boundary of a town or village under attack. How it was possible to determine which soldier was first, I don't know, but whenever possible, Moscow radio did broadcast the roll call of "firsts," and where they came from. It was a matter of tremendous pride when the native of a village or town was "first" onto the German defenses.

Dr. Gurevitch came rubbing his hands with glee. "I am very happy and very proud to tell you that I am in a position to reveal who was 'first' in the assault on Odessa, and where he came from."

"Oh, we all know," said one of the guests, "it had to be someone from Odessa."

"With all due respect to your 'rodina'," said Dr. Gurevitch, "I did say I was both proud and happy. It was one of our lads from Irkutsk that did it. I could tell from his regiment. It was originally formed in Irkutsk to fight in the civil war."

A great cheer rose from the guests who hailed from Irkutsk on Siberia's Lake Baikal.

"And his name?" asked my grandmother, her arm affectionately round my grandfather's waist. "We want to drink to him, to all those he loves, all those who love him."

Perhaps I had better say that in those days and times one never heard anything very clearly on the radio. There was static, crackles, interference. Governments did not have to jam broadcasts. Nature and the quality of reception did it adequately enough for them.

"I think I've got the name right," said Dr. Gurevitch. And he gave the soldier's name.

It took a minute or two for the room to hush. I didn't know it at the time, still being young, and it was all explained to me much later, but the soldier's surname was also my mother's maiden name. It is quite an unusual surname. She was born in a hamlet outside Irkutsk, but she and all her brothers and sisters had gone to school there. It is, after all, the capital of Siberia. As far as we knew, her family were all in the Red Army, even her oldest sister. There had always been friendly rivalry between the Jews of Odessa on the Black Sea and the Jews of Irkutsk on Lake Baikal. It was just the sort of oneupmanship one would expect from a Siberian Jew towards the ones from Odessa. Be first into Odessa, past the German defenses, just to show that boastful lot who came from there. It was worth risking one's life for.

"Did he live?"

"I don't know," said Dr. Gurevitch, "but his name and origin are not in doubt. I can put my hand on my heart and swear to that."

Everyone present knew how bad things were between my mother and grandmother. Grandmother was a jealous and possessive woman. She never forgave Mother for marrying her only son. In her heart of hearts she never forgave her that this much-loved son died. When I was older, I heard stories that she had treated Mother badly when she was widowed and had been unkind when she held the whiphand over her financially. She had not forgiven Mother for marrying again. Grandmother resented Mother's progressive ideas, her refusal to observe the old customs and traditions, her modernism. Mother considered her former mother-in-law from her first marriage ignorant and superstitious. Mother had been to university. She spoke foreign languages. Grandmother was illiterate. She had be taught to recite her prayers by heart.

Everyone present knew the imperfection of radio reception. In those days imagination filled in what did not come through in a purely technical sense. The suspicion was that Dr. Gurevitch had invented all this for the sake of bringing peace to the family. If a member of my mother's family, no matter how far removed, had been first into Odessa when it was liberated, this would put my grandmother in her debt not only in this life, but in the life to come.

Dr. Gurevitch would not be shaken in his testimony.

Grandmother kept a jewel box by her bedside. She went to it now and draped its contents over her hand, scooping up the rest in her palm. She had never visited us without an invitation formally delivered from Mother. Now she went unannounced and uninvited, her hands dripping precious necklaces and brooches.

The guests followed and I went along wide-eyed. It is one of the earliest scenes I remember from my childhood. Much of its significance was then lost on me. The dramatic impact was overwhelming.

The cook opened the door and seeing the crowd, most of them quite drunk, fled to fetch Mother.

Mother came to the door and froze, one eyebrow lifted, head tilted in disapproval, her tiny figure blocking the way.

As far back as Biblical times, in fact, in the time of Ezra (we are told), benedictions were instituted and formulated either as part of worship or to be uttered on special occasions. "Blessed be the Lord our God, King of the Universe, Who has granted me the fruit of the vine," says a good Jew over his first drink of the day. "Blessed be the Lord Who has granted me the pleasure of seeing such a lovely face," says a rabbinical student, chatting up a pretty girl. "Blessed be He, Who has saved me from a rotten deal," Grandfather would often say when he had had a narrow escape from some minor commercial disaster. There are benedictions for every possible occasion and you can make them up as you go along, so long as you know the formula.

My mother wouldn't know how to recite a benediction if you gave her the latest book on rationalist philosophy for a prize. But she can recognize one.

Grandmother lifted her hands like a priest. Precious stones shimmered.

"Blessed be the Lord our God," she began.

Mother's eyebrows began to come together.

"...King of the Universe..."

"Is anything the matter?" Mother began, now looking concerned. Had the old lady flipped?

"Ssssh!" said someone. "It isn't done to interrupt a benediction."

My grandmother completed the benediction. I don't remember what it was, but for a long time afterwards, neighbors asked Grandmother to recite it for them to write down and repeat.

Then Grandmother put her pearl necklace around Mother's throat, and followed it with a diamond necklace held by a jeweled clasp. She pinned on Mother's breast the diamond brooch that Grandfather had given her for their silver wedding anniversary. She took my mother's unwilling hand and put a bracelet on it. It had belonged to her own mother and it had come from Odessa. Mother hated jewelry. She stood there perplexed, trying not to display any emotion. One or two drunken voices began to shout explanations. Mother wasn't very tolerant of drunks, either.

Grandmother, having put her own mother's bracelet round my mother's wrist, kissed her hand reverently. Too late Mother realized what the old lady was doing. She snatched it away as if it had been scalded.

At this Grandmother broke down. She began to weep. "Forgive me," she sobbed. "Forgive me for everything."

Of course, Mother forgave her nothing.

Many years later my sister-in-law, who had the events described to her by her mother, who had been present, explained to me what my mother must have felt: that it was bad enough not to be accepted because of her marriages, to be disliked and resented for no reason to do with one's character or personality. It was even worse to be accepted eventually not for one's own sake, but for the sake of an unknown relative whose name had come over radio static.

But not even my mother could return the gifts Grandmother brought that day. So she declared she would keep them in trust for the girl my brother would one day marry. When I heard this, I protested. Why was I to be excluded? Was she not my grandmother, too?

That is when I learnt the bitter truth. These were not my real grandparents. They were my half-brother's grandparents, but not mine. At night I cried into my pillow with rage and frustration. I loved them both dearly, and however they had felt towards my mother, they treated me as flesh and blood. Besides, neither Mother nor Father seemed to want to share their own parents with me. Mother said she had no idea where her parents came from, but wherever it was, it had certainly not been Odessa. Father said he'd never asked. He hadn't thought it would ever matter to anyone. What difference did it make where one came from?

My Tientsin grandfather, the one from Odessa, heard about my unsuccessful research into the family's past. He took me on his knee. "We are the only grandparents you will ever have. Give me a hug. And now, a hug for your granny." It was a Friday night. The Sabbath candles were lit and there was a huge chocolate cake on the table. Mother never lit the Sabbath candles. We only had chocolate cake when there were visitors.

The civil war came to China. Whatever it was that came to my sister-in-law, it wasn't Grandmother's jewels.

As for me, I have been lucky. I have survived war and revolution, adopted and discarded several passports as I crossed and recrossed frontiers.

"Where do you come from?" people now ask me. "Deep down inside you, is there a country you consider your own?"

My country is Odessa.

Alex Auswaks, who comes from China, now lives in an old house in St. Albans where he writes stories dealing mainly with politics and the occult, as well as crime novels. He commutes to London daily to lecture on linguistics.

"What he told me revealed an aspect of Smith of which I had had no inkling."

The Bore

BY E.G. CHIPULINA

DESPITE its fine Norman church which rises in splendid isolation from a hill behind the main cluster of houses, strictly speaking Hornbourne is scarcely more than a hamlet. A leisurely stream, parts of which are almost entirely covered with watercress, flows parallel to the only street in a series of shallow steps that make the sound of gently cascading water one of the most attractive features of the place. The Thames is not far, the nearest town being Wallingford, and a mile or so to the east, the land begins to rise towards the Chilterns. There is much agricultural activity in the countryside around, but if Hornbourne was once involved in it, today it holds itself distinctly aloof. The only genuinely rural folk to be seen about are laborers from nearby farms who occasionally frequent the public bar at the White Hart.

Vintage houses predominate: Tudor, Elizabethan, Jacobean, all meticulously preserved, so that an illusion of unspoilt rural serenity prevails. Yet everything strikes the eye as just that little bit too neat and tidy, too freshly painted, and it does not take a great deal of imagination to visualize what elaborate *mod cons* those venerable façades conceal.

About my fellow villagers, if I may so call them, I know precious little. It's not that they are essentially unsociable, but the majority seem to be commuting business people who probably regard Hornbourne primarily as a retreat from the bustle and the pressures of the City market place where, incidentally, judging by the shiny limousines to be glimpsed through a discreet camouflage of weeping willows, most of them do not seem to have done too badly. I don't mean that we are all stockbrokers—there are others, retired folk like my wife and me—but all in all there is a definite odor of money about the place. Nor do I mean that people are necessarily stand-offish; in fact, the White Hart is widely patronized and on most evenings hums with animated small talk.

For all its hackneyed name, the White Hart is a veritable little gem, with its very low crossbeams and narrow wooden benches along the recesses of its latticed windows. Strangers are by no means uncommon: people from the married quarters of a nearby RAF base, or the occasional passing motorist, as the sign is visible from the main road. There are also a few semi-regulars who live in the area—like Smith.

Smith has been coming in on most Saturday evenings for the past several years. A widower, he lives some ten miles away near Abingdon, and his main weekend diversion is to roam the countryside in his mini, usually rounding off an afternoon with a visit to the White Hart. Everyone knows and has a word for Smith, but at the same time most people will skillfully avoid being cornered by him because however civil and amiable he may be, he is also something of a bore. Personally I find it very difficult to avoid him, possibly because I happen to be one of those unfortunate people who, if I made my analogy clear, are easily pressured into buying things they do not want. But on the other hand he is about my own age; I doubt if he has many friends, and he seems to have a special predilection for my company; so I can hardly be so uncharitable as to begrudge him an occasional hour or two—less so ever since, quite by chance, I learnt the details of his strange problem.

Before that I didn't know a great deal about Smith, except that he seemed to have an inordinate passion for all things military, that he worked in a library where he must have imbibed all the literature on the subject that came his way—I mean I've heard him quoting Liddell-Hart as glibly as a clergyman from the Bible—that he was fond of potted plants and, of course, the countryside. Once, having met him by chance in Abingdon, I had been lured to his lodgings—the only time I have been there—with the promise of being shown "something very special," which proved to be a truly amazing collection of military badges, buttons and suchlike, all highly polished and beautifully displayed in glass cases. It was not his hobby, however, that made him a bore—after all, collecting military insignia is much like any other—nor even the half-digested military wisdom that he freely dispensed, but rather a sort of exaggerated patriotism that he was wont to express in utterances such as, "I can never understand why people insist on going abroad for their holidays with all this glorious countryside on their doorstep! We fought the war to preserve it, and the way of life that is a part of it, didn't we?" Even those who might be inclined to agree with him were put off not only by something essentially cranky about him but by his constant allusions to the war, especially his own part in it. Whether those who heard him happened to be men who had done their fair share of fighting or spent the war behind a desk, Smith seemed to have discovered a way of rubbing both the wrong way with a single stroke.

Somehow he always seemed to become less assertive when he was alone with me for awhile. I believe the reason was that he had made up his mind that I held him in high esteem, and therefore no longer found it necessary to blow his military trumpet at me. In fact, he could be quite pleasant to talk to when he chatted about his work, his geraniums, or perhaps some delightful inn he had discovered tucked away in an unexpected corner, and the fidgety little gestures of his hands and elbows that usually punctuated his more jingoistic noises vanished altogether.

One Saturday afternoon when Smith and I happened to be the first arrivals at the White Hart, two youths came in, walked up to the bar and self-consciously asked for two pints of bitter. The landlady, a lean schoolmarmish sort of woman, fixed them with a penetrating look. "Now, honestly, you aren't eighteen yet, are you?" The youths eyed each other sheepishly, stood their ground for a moment, then walked out without a word.

Smith nodded sagely. "Spoilt generation, if you ask me! Not their fault, I suppose. Too much money to spend, don't you agree?"

Before he could warm to his theme, a man called Byrne, whom I knew by sight, walked in with a tall, gray-haired stranger.

"You're a hard woman, Molly," said Byrne teasingly.

"I don't care," retorted the landlady. "I'm not risking my license for the likes of them. Where in heaven's name do they come from? I have them in here every other day!"

"Now, now," said Byrne. "Don't start getting all worked up so early—it's a long evening. Usual for me, please, and I believe it's a Scotch-and-water for Mr. Stanton here."

I realized that Smith was craning his neck, trying to see round me, as I was leaning on the counter between him and the two men. "Stanton?" he repeated. "Did he say Stanton?"

The stranger, hearing his name, glanced across. "Yes?"

I stepped back a little, and then noticed the curious, half-anxious expression on Smith's face as he gazed at the stranger's. "Captain...Stanton," he said, but I'm not sure whether as a statement or a question.

The stranger smiled. "You're going back a bit, aren't you?"

"Back?" Smith looked away, absently entwining his fingers round the tankard in front of him. There followed an awkward silence, during which I noticed that a sickly pallor was creeping into Smith's face, and that his brow was furrowed as if he were in pain.

I laid a hand on his arm. "Is something the matter, Tom?"

Stanton said hesitantly, "I'm sorry, I don't quite..."

"Clarençon," said Smith, but he seemed to be talking to himself.

"Come on!" said Stanton soothingly. "Not much point in raking up all that now, is there? Let me buy you a drink."

Smith, seeming not to hear, relaxed his grip on the tankard and, murmuring excuses, went off in the direction of the toilet.

Stanton watched the receding figure dubiously. "Is he all right, d'you think?"

Byrne, who had just returned from a brief flutter on the fruit machine in the corner, said flippantly: "What's wrong with old Smithy, had one too many?"

"Smith!" said Stanton. "That's a help!"

"You don't remember him?" I said.

Stanton shook his head. "But that place he mentioned... Clarençon..."

"That's right. Does it mean anything?"

Stanton moved his head doubtfully. "Depends on how you look at it. Bloody awful mess."

"Normandy?"

"Yes. They caught us with our pants down. SS tanks. We had no air cover because of the weather, no anti-tank weapons either. I'm not sure there were many survivors from that show; I got through by the skin of my teeth anyhow."

"Oh, come on!" pleaded Byrne. "We get enough of that from Smith!"

Stanton laughed good-naturedly. The conversation took a turn, and after awhile it struck me that Smith was taking a long time. I excused myself and went to check in case he was ill, but there was no sign of him in the toilet, and when I went outside to see if he had gone for a breather, I noticed that his mini was no longer where I had seen him park. Reasoning that if he were capable of driving he couldn't be feeling all that bad, I left it at that. But it wasn't like Smith to go off without a word, and later a lingering uneasiness made me look through the telephone directory. But if he had a 'phone it must have been in his landlady's name, and I had no idea what it was.

About noon the following day, I went into the White Hart to buy cigarettes and found a well-dressed, middle-aged man with thick spectacles in earnest conversation with the landlady who, on catching sight of me, interrupted him.

"Wait a minute," she said. "Mr. Smith was standing right here with you last night, if I remember right."

The stranger turned round to look at me. "Ah, are you an acquaintance of his, perhaps?"

"Yes. I've known him for years—comes in here most

Saturdays."

"Yes, I'm aware of that. Do you have any idea if anything happened last night that might have upset him?"

"Well, evidently something did." I described the incident. "It must have brought back some unpleasant experience, I suppose, but then...he's always talking about the war, you know. Are you his friend, by the way?"

"Yes. I'm also his doctor."

"Oh? Is he ill, then?"

The doctor hesitated, as if reluctant to discuss the matter.

"I *am* his friend too, you know," I said, introducing myself. "Perhaps I could be of some help." I confess that my genuine concern was tinged with curiousity.

The doctor seemed to reconsider his attitude. "Yes, I'm sorry, you're probably right. My name is Foster, David Foster. Could we...?" He indicated a corner table.

"By all means. But let me get you a drink first."

As we talked in relative privacy, Foster did not seem at all surprised at how little I knew about Smith's past or background despite my having known him for so long. What he told me revealed an aspect of Smith of which I had had no inkling.

My own private, and humble, opinion about human attitudes towards war is that, except for committed idealists or those daredevils who seem to derive pleasure from danger, most men go reluctantly, even if dutifully. The optimist may feel convinced that he will scrape through somehow or at least get a lucky wound, but still he has no delusions that it will be a picnic, while the pessimist, like Caesar's cowards, will die many times. Probably the less imaginative, not being so prone to visions of anticipated horrors or to relive past experience, adapt to the situation better than most. But they are all potential heroes—or potential cowards—and what binds them together in a cohesive unit is not merely discipline, but, I believe, basically the same invisible agent that keeps most of society in line—regard for what the neighbors will think.

I'm still not sure where, even in the light of Foster's tale, Smith fits into all this. That he was imaginative in his youth there seems to be no doubt. But what went on in his mind? How did he visualize war? According to Foster he had spent his boyhood in Aldershot, where his father owned a bookshop. If this had not actually engendered, it must have at least stimulated his consuming passion for the army: its panoply, its traditions and mystique. When war came he must have suffered agonies of impatience because he was still too young to enlist. But the war dragged on obligingly and in 1943 his dream came true—the vast human sacrifice that its realization had entailed probably never crossed his mind. Eventually, he was posted to an infantry regiment training in the north of England for the coming invasion, and his letters home at the time, lovingly preserved by his mother, suggested that those may have been the happiest days of his life.

When he heard the long-awaited news of D-day, one can imagine his disappointment at having missed out, for his unit was evidently being held in reserve. His turn came when the fighting around Caen threatened to grind to a stalemate. For a week or so his first taste of war seems to have been limited to the distant rumble of artillery. Unfortunately, when it came, his first baptism of fire proved to be no mere sprinkling but—if such a metaphor is at all appropriate—a total immersion. The weather had been consistently foul for days, and with the air force grounded the Germans were enjoying an unwonted freedom of movement. A section of Smith's company, moving slowly on the road to a village called Clarençon, suddenly took the brunt of a surprise attack by heavy tanks, and it seems that one of the first shells exploded very close to Smith, literally blowing his immediate comrades to pieces. Perhaps if Smith had been hit too, this tale might have been called "The Short and Happy Life of Thomas Smith" but Smith, shocked and deafened though he must have been, emerged miraculously unscathed. What passed through Smith's mind during those moments—if indeed anything did—it would be pretentious to divine. But whether as a result of mentation or sheer animal instinct, it is certain that he ran, ran as fast and as far as his legs could carry him, and they seem to have carried him to some derelict farmhouse where he hid himself. There, eventually, a German patrol discovered him, and the soldiers, probably hardened veterans, evidently jeered at him on finding that his weapon had not been fired. In being taken prisoner, he seems to have retraced his steps, crossing the very road that was still littered with the remains of his comrades. He spent the rest of the war in a POW camp.

Foster had told me his story with the air of a man with an intimate knowledge of his subject, but when he returned after fetching a round of drinks, he said: "Mind you, most of what I've told you about Tom I only know at second hand, from his parents when they were alive, and mainly from his late wife, a sensitive and understanding woman. This...breakdown, you might call it, that he's going through now—it's happened before, you know. Many years ago in London he ran into a man who had been with him in the POW camp."

"I'm sure you're right," I interrupted, "but it doesn't seem to make sense. I mean, I can understand these chance meetings bringing back to him all that horror and humiliation, but then why does he keep harping on the war?"

"I'm afraid it's not very simple. Let me try to explain. I managed to trace this fellow-POW he met in London, Gregg was the name. Fortunately an intelligent and compassionate man, and what I learnt from him about Tom proved extremely helpful. At first, he told me, he had thought Tom was just a naïve young show-off, with all his irritating blather about the tight—and by implication, heroic—situations he had been in. But Gregg slept next to him and soon became aware that Tom was plagued by a recurring nightmare during which he seemed to relive with extraordinary clarity the events I've just told you about. The next thing he discovered was that Tom seemed to remember nothing at all about these dreams. Moreover, when he tried to help him to remember, Tom appeared to make a serious effort, but all that happened was that he became ill and depressed. For awhile the whole thing baffled Gregg; but, as I said, he was no fool, and gradually he came to the conclusion that Tom not only couldn't recall his dream but sincerely believed every detail of his seemingly cock-and-bull stories of heroics. Of course he had heard of amnesia and that sort of thing, and rightly imagined Tom's case to be some variant of the same trouble. He had no idea if anything could be done to help him, but from then on, without saying a word to anyone, he did his best to shield Tom from the banter and the ridicule that he unwittingly brought upon himself."

I said, "What happened, then, when Tom recognized this fellow, what's his name...Stanton? Do you think it all came back suddenly?"

Foster shook his head. "So far as I know he's quite incapable of recalling the repressed experience, no matter how hard he tries. You see, it's not a conscious evasion but some kind of protective mechanism that seems to block a memory which is too painful to his self-esteem—something that perhaps he couldn't live with. But you know the old saying: 'Can't get something for nowt.' The repressing may be an unconscious process but evidently it's continuous, imposing a strain on the system. When he recognized Stanton he was probably making a genuine effort to recall the circumstances, and something must have given way."

"It all sounds terribly complicated," I said. "Isn't there any treatment?"

"There are ways and means—drugs, hypnotism. But I suppose it's a long and costly process."

"Are you a psychiatrist, by the way?"

"No, I'm a physician. I merely pick the brains of my psychiatrist friends."

"Don't you think Tom should see a psychiatrist?"

Foster laughed dryly. "Just mention the word, psychiatrist, to Tom!" His voice half-heartedly mimicked Tom's. "'Nobody's going to tamper with *me*!' Reminds me of a certain type of married man when you have to recommend a fertility check-up."

"Yes," I mused, "I can imagine. But...will it never come back to him, then?"

"I'm not sure. I believe there have been cases of spontaneous recollection. There's no doubt that the memory is there somewhere, as those nightmares show. I suppose they still recur now and then, but I no longer have any means of knowing, ever since his wife died."

By the following weekend Smith had resumed his old routine. Not a word from him about the incident with Stanton, though I naturally forbore to mention it.

He seems pretty much his old self again, but I find that I have become more aware of his oddities, and the usual leg-pulling or the generally good-natured wisecracks they make behind his back tend to irritate me now. I often wonder what sort of person he might have been if the heroics of his fantasies had really taken place.

E.G. Chipulina, a full-time short-story writer with a strong interest in history, also writes novels, and short stories for children. His work has been published for 25 years, mostly on the Continent. His stories have also appeared in previous issues of SSI. Mr. Chipulina's love of language and literature is closely matched by a love of painting and sketching.

"Got cold feet, have you?"

The Swim

BY DEZSŐ KOSZTOLÁNYI

THE sun was white-hot in the sky.

In the harsh light the Balaton bathing resort glittered dazzlingly, as when flash-powder ignites to take pictures in the dark. Within the compass of the whitewashed cabins, the maize sheds, and the sand, everything seemed white. Even the sky. The dusty leaves of the acacia trees were as white as blotting paper.

It was about half past two in the afternoon.

On this day Suhajda had eaten an early lunch. Now he came down the porch steps into the flower garden bordering the cottage yard.

"Where are you going?" asked Mrs. Suhajda, crocheting among the sweet williams.

"Bathing," yawned Suhajda, a pair of cherry-red bathing trunks dangling from his hand.

"Take him with you," Mrs. Suhajda pleaded.

"No."

"Why not?"

"Because he doesn't deserve it," Suhajda replied. "Because he's a lazy good-for-nothing." He paused. "Because he won't work."

"But he does," protested his wife, shrugging her shoulders. "He studied all morning."

On the bench in front of the kitchen a boy of eleven pricked up his ears. A closed book rested in his lap: his Latin grammar.

He was a thin child with hair cropped close, in a red gym vest, duck trousers, and leather sandals on his feet. He squinted towards his mother and father.

"Well," Suhajda said gruffly, throwing back his stern head to stare at the boy, "how do you say: 'I shall be praised?'"

"Lauderentur," faltered the boy without thinking, but first he got to his feet, like in school.

"Lauderentur," nodded his father contemptuously, "lauderentur. So you're going to fail your second examination too."

"He knows it," his mother appealed. "He does know it, he's just confused. You make him flustered."

"I shall take him out of school," Suhajda said, egging himself on. "I will too, so help me God. I'll apprentice him to a locksmith—a cartwright." He did not know himself what made him choose those particular trades in his fit of passion, trades he ordinarily never even thought of.

"Come here, Jancsika," his mother called. "You'll be a good boy and work hard, won't you, Jancsika?"

"That brat will be the death of me yet," broke in Suhajda, because anger was like spice to him, adding relish to his days. "He'll be the death of me yet," he repeated, reveling in the salutary effect of the fury coursing through his veins, dilating them, dispelling the dullness of the afternoon.

"I'll work hard," the boy stammered inaudibly.

In his humble insignificance he stole a look at his mother, seeking protection.

He barely saw his father. Was just aware of his presence. Of his odious presence, everywhere, at all times.

"Don't bother," said Suhajda, with a deprecating gesture of the hand. "Why should you? It's not worth it."

"He shall work hard," his mother said, hugging the boy's head to her and caressing him. "And you will forgive him. Jancsika," she said abruptly, "go and fetch your bathing trunks, there's a good boy. Your father is going to take you swimming."

Jancsi could not conceive what had happened, what lay behind his mother's intervention which had arbitrarily and with miraculous rapidity ended the contention between them. But he dashed up the porch steps into the small dark cubbyhole of a room to search for his swimming trunks in all the drawers. They were cherry-red, just like his father's, only smaller. His mother had sewn them both.

The father seemed to waver.

Without saying a word to his wife he stopped by a gooseberry bush, apparently waiting for his tarrying son. Then he must have changed his mind. He walked out through the lattice-gate and set off towards the lake, at a somewhat slower pace than usual.

The boy rummaged for a long time.

Jancsi was in the second form at grammar school and had failed Latin at the end of the year. He had to spend the summer vacation preparing to resit the examination, but as he made light of studying even during the holidays his father had forbidden bathing for a week as a punishment. There were two days of that week still to go. This was an opportunity too good to be missed. He turned out his drawers feverishly, scattering his clothes all over the floor. At last he found his trunks. He did not stop to stuff them in a bag, just ran out into the yard, brandishing them triumphantly. Only his mother was out there waiting for him. He stood on tiptoe to breathe a hasty kiss on that sweet, adorable cheek, then raced off after his father.

His mother called after him that she would be coming down to join them later.

Suhajda was walking about twenty paces ahead of him down the path. Jancsi's sandals beat up little clouds of dust as he ran. He caught up with his father by the box-thorn hedge. But when there were no more than a couple of steps between them he slowed his pace and crept alongside him warily like a dog, afraid he might be chased off after all.

The father did not speak. His face, which the child would scout with quick, sidelong glances every now and then, was stony and inscrutable. He walked with his head thrown back, staring into space. He looked as though he had not even noticed his son's presence, as if he could not care less that he was there.

Jancsi, who had been full of joy at his good fortune only a moment ago, was now crestfallen. He ambled dejectedly beside his father, feeling thirsty, wanting a drink, wanting to relieve himself; he would have liked to turn back but was afraid that his father would berate him for it and so had to accept the situation he had created by joining his father through fear of another even worse.

He waited to see what would happen to him.

To walk from the summer cottages to the lake did not take more than four minutes.

It was a miserable place, this resort, on the shingled southern shores of the lake, with no electric light and no conveniences, distinctly third-rate. Poor office clerks spent their vacations here, people who could afford nothing better.

In the yard beneath the mulberry trees sat women and men wearing nothing but a shirt, munching hot corn on the cob and slices of watermelon.

Suhajda greeted his acquaintances in his customary affable manner, from which his son deduced—during this blissful period of truce—that he could not be as angry as he had been making out. Later, though, his father's brow darkened once more and his face resumed its fierce, forbidding expression.

Crickets chirred in the sunshine. The cloying, putrid smell of the water was in their nostrils, the tumble-down bath hut had come in sight but still Suhajda did not speak.

Mrs. Istenes, the bath attendant, who wore a red kerchief tied around her bun, opened their huts for them. Into the first she ushered Suhajda; into the second, which Mrs. Suhajda used for changing, she let in the boy.

Apart from them the shore was deserted except for a young lad busily working on a rickety old boat. He was straightening rusty nails out on the ground.

Jancsi was first to get changed.

He came out of his hut but did not know what to do with himself. He dared not go into the much-coveted water. In his confusion he stared at his feet. He stared at them attentively, as though he were seeing them for the first time, until his father was ready.

Suhajda stepped out of his hut in his cherry-red trunks, slightly potbellied, but still muscular and strong, his hairy chest laid bare, the black bushiness of which always made his son stare.

Jancsi glanced up at him, trying to read his mood from his eyes, but he could see nothing written there. The gold-rimmed pince-nez flashed too brightly in the sun.

He looked on bashfully as his father entered the water.

He did not sidle after him until Suhajda had called over his shoulder:

"Come on!"

He followed him into the water, always one step behind. He did not dive or duck or paddle as he usually did. He just stumbled along in his father's wake waiting for some kind of encouragement. Suhajda sensed this. In a dour, contemptuous voice he asked:

"Got cold feet, have you?"

"No."

"Why're you acting like a ruddy tomfool then?"

They were standing by the pile where the water reached up to the boy's nipples and was a little higher than his father's waist. They both squatted down until it came up to their necks, luxuriating in the languid caresses of the tepid water which frothed creamily, apple-green around them.

The pleasantness of it buoyed up Suhajda's spirits. He began to chaff the child:

"I think you are scared, my friend."

"No."

But he had already caught up his son in his arms and had hurled him into the water.

Jancsi soared in the air. He landed backside first with a splash. The waters parted, then, foaming, with a mysterious rushing sound, closed above his head. It took him a few seconds to come up again. Water spurted from his nose and mouth. He rubbed his eyes with his fists because he couldn't see straight away.

"Was it bad?" his father asked.

"No."

"Then let's do it again. One—two—" and he gathered the boy up in his arms again.

At the count of "three" Suhajda swung the boy high and sent him flying into the water to land at approximately the same spot he had landed before, a little farther off though, behind the pile to which the ropes were attached, and so did not see that the boy, turning a somersault in the air, had fallen into the water with his head thrown back and his arms spread wide. So he turned.

Opposite stretched the Somogy shore. The lake shimmered in the sunshine as though millions and millions of butterflies were beating its surface with diamond wings.

For a few second he waited, as he had before.

"Hey," he said at last, nettled.

Then, hoarsely, menacingly:

"Stop playing the fool now! Cut it out!"

But no one answered him.

"Where are you?" he asked in a somewhat louder voice, peering ahead and back, a long way out with his myopic eyes, in case the boy had come up there, farther out, for Jancsi could swim excellently underwater too.

But while Suhajda was doing all this, he sensed that Jancsi had been underwater for a long time, longer than during his previous dive. Much longer.

He was stricken with terror.

He jumped up, hurtling headlong through the water towards the spot where his son had presumably landed.

And as he waded he kept shouting:

"Jancsi, Jancsi!"

At that spot he did not find him behind the pile either. So he began to churn the water with his arms, flailing them like paddles. He raked near the surface and down deep, fitfully, erratically; he tried to make out the lake bed but the turbid water did not allow his gaze to penetrate further than a span. He ducked his head, which he had so far kept dry, under water, eyes goggling behind his pince-nez like those of a fish. He searched for his son, searched on his elbows, squatting on his heels, diving again and again, spinning round and round, bending to one side, systematically keeping count of every inch of covered ground.

But his son was nowhere to be found.

There was just the water, the terrifying sameness of the water everywhere.

He staggered to his feet, retching, and took a deep breath.

While underwater, he had formed a vague hope that his son would have surfaced while he was still down below; that he would be standing, laughing before the pile or even further off by the time he rose; that he would perhaps even have run back to the hut to change.

But now he knew that however long the time may have seemed to him, he had not been underwater for more than a few moments, and that his son could not have left the lake.

Above the water a scene of such tranquility, of such indifference greeted him as he had never before thought imaginable.

"Hey!" he bellowed towards the shore and did not recognize his own voice, "I can't find him anywhere!"

The young lad who was caulking the boat cupped his hand against his ear.

"What?"

"I can't find him anywhere!"

In his desperation the words rattled in his throat.

"Who?"

"I can't find him!" He roared at the top of his voice, "Help!"

The lad placed his hammer on the rower's seat, kicked off his trousers—he did not want to get them wet—and slipped into the water. He began to run as fast as he could but still he seemed to be taking his time. Waiting for the boy to arrive Suhajda dove under another couple of times, kneeling in the water, scrambling on all fours to look for his son in other directions, then, alarmed by the distance he had covered, returned to the spot he had been standing sentinel over. He held on to the pile so he would not faint.

By the time the lad got there Suhajda was dazedly gasping for breath. He could not give an intelligible answer to the young man's questions.

They both wandered around uncertainly.

On the shore Mrs. Istenes was wringing her hands.

In answer to her cries about twenty or thirty people had gathered, bringing grappling hooks and nets, and even a rowing boat had set out towards the scene of the accident, which was really quite unnecessary, as the water was too shallow at that spot to cover anybody.

Soon the rumor was going around that "Someone had drowned." As a fact.

At that moment, in the flower garden among the sweet wiliams, Mrs. Suhajda put down her crocheting. She got up, went into the small dark room where Jancsika had looked for his bathing trunks, then, locking the door behind her, set off for the shore, as she had promised him.

She strolled slowly beneath her parasol, which served to protect her from the fierce rays of the sun. She wondered whether she should bathe or not. She decided she would not bathe that day. But when she reached the boxthorn hedge the chain of her thoughts was suddenly broken, jumbled up. She closed her parasol and began to run, ran all the way until she reached the bathhouse.

There were two gendarmes standing by the bathhouse, and a mumbling crowd, mostly peasant women, many of whom were crying.

The mother realized immediately what had happened. She staggered down to the shore, wailing, towards the close group of people at the center of which lay her son. They did not allow her near. They set her down on a chair. In a swoon, she kept asking if he was alive or not.

He was not. They had found him after a quarter of an hour's search directly behind the pile which his father had guarded, and by the time they pulled him out of the water his heart had stopped beating and the sensitiveness of his pupils had ceased. The doctor stood him on his head, shook the water out of him, put a pillow under his chest, tried artificial respiration, worked the thin, dead arms up and down, up and down for a long time, then checked for heartbeats every minute with his stethoscope. But the heart did not resume its beating. He then threw his instruments into his bag and went away.

This death, which had come so suddenly, apparently through

some freakish turn of fortune, had now become a fact, as unchangeable, as unalterable and solid as the largest mountain ranges of the earth.

The mother was taken home in a cart. Suhajda was still sitting on the shore in his cherry-red bathing trunks. Water and tears streamed down his face, his pince-nez. He was heaving great, delirious sighs.

"Oh God, oh dear God."

Two people had to help him to his feet. They led him to his hut to get changed at last.

It was not yet three.

Dezső Kosztolányi, the eminent poet, short story writer, novelist, journalist and literary translator, was born into a provincial middle class family in Szabadka. He was an excellent student and gained recognition early as a writer. His short stories are outstanding pieces of the genre in Hungarian literature. At first they were concerned with the secrets of man's inner world, later on social conflicts came to the fore. This story was translated by Eszter Molnár.

"Don't, I pleaded silently as I stood tethered
to solid ground before the building."

Eye-Witness

BY DINA MEHTA

THAT Sunday as I stepped out into the high dazzle of the day from
the porch of my building, I felt blank without my glasses. And looked
it too, no doubt. My nose missed its long intimacy with steel rims,
my ears the tight hug behind them. My thick lenses were sitting out
the weekend at an oculist's where a fat man with padded palms and
conical fingertips had promised to mount them for me in the jazzy
pink frames I had selected over Aunt Roma's protests. And without
them I felt subdued, exposed. Like a tribal belle with the tattoo
marks erased from her face.

I was walking up the paved incline towards the vague green oval
of the distant lawn when a man brushed past me, almost knocking
me over, shouting, "Look up there!"

I wanted to say something rude to him. The maniac could have
maimed me for life! But he had already shot past and stood rooted
to the ground some distance away, staring up at the house and
gesticulating emphatically. So I looked up, too, but could see nothing
but the dense geometry of the eight-storied building. I shrugged, and
turned to walk on. But something held me back. I retraced my steps

towards the man who took pen-and-ink definition as Mr. Gopalan, a retired solicitor and our neighbor on the floor immediately below us. He was open-mouthed. His upturned face registered alarm.

"What is it?" I asked him.

He threw a perfunctory glance at me at his elbow. Either he did not recognize me without my spectacles or he dismissed me as a harmless hallucination in pigtails and faded denims, for he continued to stare up at the building, his hand to his mouth, his Brahmin's ample *ghee*-fed middle carelessly draped with a checkered *lungi*. He had now ceased his insane exertions and was cast in the mold of a question mark, his stomach protruding, his hirsute torso coffee-shouldered in the sun.

Again I followed his gaze up. After a long, eye-aching moment, I thought I saw a figure in blue poised on the parapet of the terrace. Was it dressed in blue? Or was I merely staring into the blue haze of the intolerable sky?

"What's the matter?" I asked again, my eyes on the sacred thread that cut across his chest. Before he could answer a man came dashing out of the building. "*Sahib,*" I heard our liftman Yakub address Mr. Gopalan, "will you phone for the police?"

"How long has she been up there?"

"She called the lift to the fourth floor an hour ago, to take her up to the terrace." Yakub was breathing heavily. "How was I to know? Will her family blame me? They did not even know she had escaped from her room till I rang at their door just now. Could I have refused to take her up?"

"Never mind that! Get back up there at once. Try to—"

"But from up only I'm coming down! The door to the terrace she's locked from inside and will not open!"

"Let me think. What about the door from the north side?"

"Mehra *sahib* has the key and he's out of town. Six o'clock this morning he left for—"

"Well break down the nearest bloody door!" Mr. Gopalan had suddenly raised his voice to a shout.

"As you say, *sahib!*"

"Take someone with you to help. Get Ramsingh up there with some tools. I'm going for the phone. Hurry!"

Both mén turned and ran into the building.

As I stood there in the full bloom of my ignorance, a knot of apprehension began to form slowly within me. I eyed the building with false insouciance. It seemed too pale, consumptive, taking a sun cure in the intense light. Was its apparent solidity deceptive? Was it going to come down? No, not even the white glare could disguise its sturdiness. It was strong and sound but...there was something aberrant about its familiar shape today and yes, it posed a *threat!* The sky was hurtingly bright. Spots of color began to dance before my eyes and I looked away.

Round me I was surprised to find people gathered in little groups and clusters. An excited hum of voices grew louder and louder. Windows were dotted with anonymous parchment faces looking out and up. The terrace parapet had acquired a stagey significance. More people began to pour out of the building. They milled round, a shifting, vagabond audience. Nervous eyes jumped in hot faces within the narrow orbit of my vision. Everybody stared up at the terrace; they did not know what the overture was about, and were asking to be told in voices which rose, with panic and a quite delirious avidity, higher and higher:

"Have the police been informed?"

"Who is it?"

"From the fourth floor? That's the cancer patient."

"You've got it wrong. The lady's been in and out of mental hospitals."

"We'll need an ambulance."

"The fire brigade, too. I'll run up and do it at once."

"No, use my phone. We are on the ground floor." Two figures detached themselves from the crowd.

"God, she'll kill herself," said a voice behind me.

"Who is it?"

"Why don't we dash up to the terrace?"

"The door's bolted from the inside."

"God, I think I know who it is—"

"Look, she's walking the parapet again. Can't someone reach her?"

"They're trying to break down the terrace door."

Fourth floor, they kept on saying the *fourth* floor. Could they mean...? A clammy chill invaded my body, as if I had just stepped into a wet swim suit.

Again I tried to see. I could discern nothing. Without my glasses I was blind. My short-sighted sense of the unbearable distance of the sky, of dim faces fading into a gray fog, made it difficult for me to breathe. But this same physical inhibition of sight seemed to lend me a new intelligence, a powerful inner vision, as if Shiva's mystic third eye had opened suddenly between my brows and in this strange flowering of omniscience I was simultaneously two people: one gazing up, the other gazing down; one a thirteen- year-old schoolgirl anchored to the earth before a brick-and-wood monster with tingling copper arteries and plastic nerves, the other walking a parapet in mid-air, intent on placing her right foot before her left, her whole woman's body aware of the sky rushing away from her at a million miles a second, aware of the speed and the void around her as a world of bright lines drawn swiftly in parallels, a vast rapid river of scintillating strokes that made her dizzy, that indecorously hurried her forward to the point where she would have to *jump.*

Don't, I pleaded silently as I stood tethered to solid ground before the building; *don't,* a girlish plea which failed to ascend to the tilting parapet where with frail hands the woman was trying to grab the earth as it spun round her. But perhaps a pitching vision of a water tank, quick glimpses of a television aerial or a pastiche of tar and concrete helped momentarily to check the wild swoop of her vertigo, for death was again a word a mile long as she resumed her precarious pacing from one end of the wall to the other.

God, was it possible that *she* was up there with such malign intent when she had been doing so well all this week? Only last Tuesday I had erupted into our living room after school, my heavy satchel bumping my posterior, ribbons missing from my plaits as usual, my specs cloudy with sweat and finger prints, to find Mother established again on the big green divan near the window.

I had stood in the middle of the room, staring at her. Why had no one told me she was coming home today? The sense of being suddenly in her presence was so overwhelming that for a moment it forbade speech and action. Then I flung my school things on the carpet, fell on my knees beside her and covered her hand with kisses.

She had smiled and wordlessly stroked my hair, while large unwilling tears gathered in the corners of her eyes. Again my sense of her miraculous presence smote me so acutely that it created a solitude in which she alone existed, while I was totally absent. Only she. I held her wasted hand tightly in mine. Had they *starved* her at the hospital? My throat ached with indignation, so that I could not speak. But surely in those moments she had learnt that I loved her?

"Thank God the parapet's quite broad," said a voice behind me.

"Not for someone who's determined to jump."

"He's got to be crazy."

"It's a *she*, not a *he*."

"How can you tell, at this distance?"

Exactly, said my foolish heart, *how can you tell?* And quickly I repudiated my earlier knowledge, cheating myself with hope. But the spasm passed. I knew. I knew with such crushing certainty that murk welled up inside me despite the vibrant noonday sun and in that moment I thought I saw my father pushing his way through the crowd. I wanted to call out to him, but my throat was stuffed with cotton wool.

An urgent male voice said, "Patkar, I'm afraid they think it is—"

"I know!" snapped the man, looking up. It did not sound like my father, but I knew it was he. The next moment I expected his calm hand to fall on my shoulder, telling me without words that everything was *all right, Asha.* That we would manage, somehow, as we had done in the past. That the woman poised up there would pull a secret ripcord to end her freefall and float to earth with the sun making a translucence of her chute; and I would wake up from this nightmare to find myself kneeling again before the living room divan, where they always brought her after each new crisis had passed.

What had precipitated the last crisis? As my eyes strained to catch another glimpse of Father, memory dredged up for me his voice asking the same question of Aunt Roma. The night before my mother's last trip to the hospital they had come to my room when they thought my brother and I were asleep, and talked in whispers.

"Why, Roma, why? Why did it have to happen again?"

My father had spoken with an unfamiliar impatience as he paced the room. With a sinking heart I realized that he was annoyed with Mother, as if he expected her, after all these years, to recognize symptoms of strain in herself and guard against them. It seemed to me that he was hardening himself against her, deliberately driving a wedge between "Mother well" and "Mother sick." If you are not a saint isn't there something unforgivable about sickness, senility, debility in those you love?

"When did you send for Dr. Wadia?" His voice was sharp as he put the question to my aunt.

"Right away." Her voice was equally curt.

"And he advises hospitalization again?" It was becoming increasingly difficult for me to distinguish between the self-protective detachment in his voice and a new coldness that had crept in. "Roma, do you realize what this means? This collapse prophesizes a new cycle, a new bout of the malady. Dear God, my poor children...Did she seem at all strange to you when she came to breakfast this morning?"

"No, she didn't." There was a sullen backflow to Aunt Roma's voice but Father did not heed it.

"Then why...*why?*" I heard the impact of his fist being driven into his open palm and wished I were fast asleep like Vikram on the opposite bed. Just then my aunt spoke in a whisper so fiercely sibilant that I flinched under my covers: "*You* know why! *You* should know, if anyone does!"

A moment of tense silence. Then my father's voice: "Roma, do you know I haven't the slightest idea what you are talking about?"

"You are a liar!" Her voice trembled in high-pitched feminine wrath. "A shameless liar!"

"You will wake up the children. I must ask you to control yourself."

"Don't take that tone with me! I am not my sister. I'm not that poor woman you've driven out of her mind!" I could feel the flint unsheathed by Aunt Roma's words abrade him so harshly that I imagined the skin peeling off my father's face.

"Roma." His voice was held on a tight leash.

But she went on: "You think we don't know what is going on? You think we don't know about that—your woman?"

Muffled, as if speech caused him effort, Father said, "From what you are saying I presume you are referring to Gita Seth." I tensed in bed. It was he who had crystallized the situation by mentioning a name. Plump Gita took dictation from him and filed his office correspondence. He went on after another difficult pause: "People see what they choose to see. But I would like to remind you that Miss Seth came to work for me five years *after* the sickness had taken root in your sister."

Was there a plea in his last words? Was he excusing himself for an inadmissable weakness? Was there a new note in my father's voice, the voice I wished to remain unalterable forever, for if ever it *did* change I would be hurled into chaos? There must have been something in his words to menace my image of him, for that night a new dread entered my heart. Had I been betrayed? And was there something in Father to be despised?

I looked round for him in the crowd, but I had lost him. No, that was he, rushing violently into the building again, his footsteps echoing on the hard ground. I wanted to, but could not follow him. There were sly, tentative movements in the crowd towards me now, side-glances, nudges; but no one approached me. As in a dream no face beckoned me and I could reach out to no one, nothing.

I found I was biting my hand. Somewhere in the swimming green foliage an ambushed bird began to give out its piercing, reiterated notes. As they ceased the figure on the parapet must have moved spectacularly, endangering her vital balance, for I sensed the shudder that went through the crowd. A boy began to cry. Vikram? No, he was spending the weekend with our cousins in Bandra. I tried to look up again and saw two windows where I knew there was only one, saw the little curling veins my eyes projected on the blue air before they closed against the platinum light. They opened again on my grandmother's ravaged face three paces away from me. But I knew I was mistaken. *Dadima* had died a year ago.

Now there was a commotion near the rectangular space between the gate and the outskirts of the lawn. With a loud grinding an ambulance backed far in to within a few feet of where I stood. I did not move, but the crowd parted before it like blundering cattle, then became static again. Three men jumped down from the vehicle, then stood there, staring, useless. A group of curious stragglers had wandered in from the road despite the main gate being roped off by two policemen. A police constable was bundling them out again. A man behind me was actually taking photographs, his camera making amiable clicking sounds as it recorded—what? The performance on the high wall? Impossible, from this distance. The audience, then? The building? My fear, that smelled so hot in the sun?

What followed I remember with confusion. That was my house standing there, and though I was straining myopically at a relief map of balconies, grills, pipes, air conditioners, wash lines...they all hung before me in the flat dimensions of a poster, which bulged and dimpled as the woman walked the parapet. She was pursued by invisible demons, I knew, tracked by hounds, while faint sounds from below tried to claw their way up to her: the crowd sounds, the traffic sounds, the bird sounds, the knocking on doors, the hammering on doors, the tearing of wood, the hum of the elevator...

Ah, someone had mounted the last flight of stairs to the terrace. Someone was coming for her in evil haste and again there was an ugly sliding to everything. Again all was sneeringly and debasingly caricatured as with a queer rising disgust at the back of her mind, almost on the back of her tongue, she saw herself as the thing-to-be-destroyed. Ended. Her effacement was a *must*. They had entered her skull, explored each memory to its last lair—such a monstrous invasion of privacy! And now was she expected to crawl back the long way to recovery? Can a path of agony be walked again and again? When all had been tried and all had failed, her obliteration was not to be shirked. Coldly and inimically she understood this. Jump she must, eight stories down. Where a crowd churned to watch the power of destruction. Down where in my denim jeans I stood pinned to the ground by a mountain of sensations and where suddenly a woman began to pray: Old Mrs. Vaz, who looked like my grandmother.

Old Mrs. Vaz alone had the courage to acknowledge young Asha Patkar with a trembling touch on her head, before she began to mutter a Christian prayer aloud. So I, too, closed my useless eyes and from under my clenched lids voiceless crimson prayers rose compacted with her words, sent out in terror to a faceless Third Person, imploring Him to do something. But He was a complete stranger and stone deaf.

With a sudden and heart-stopping cry the woman threw herself down from the parapet.

I opened my eyes and thought I saw her go over, head down. I felt the ugly physical sensation of a sharp drop, the treacherous hole opening beneath her, the betrayal of the wind as it disavowed its burden and she landed with an unearthly sound close to where the ambulance was parked.

Everyone began running to and fro, cannoning into each other. Dismayed cries arose, then a new strange sound, as if a number of people were summoning enough breath for a yell which never came.

As the crowd closed in upon the place where my mother had fallen, with a furious clanging of bells a red truck drove in at a reckless speed and braked near the ambulance. The helmeted firemen jumped down—and did nothing. The sleeping ladder and the water hoses, slack and coiled, remained stationary above the wheels.

I stood where I was, petrified by what I had witnessed. In every bone of my body I felt the fragility of that broken body, and between my bones and the clothes I wore there was nothing. No flesh, no blood. And still over the years a part of me is impaled to that spot by the limitless volume of my loss.

Dina Mehta holds a degree in English literature from Bombay University. Her short stories are published in India, England, Holland, Australia, South Africa, Hong Kong and the USA. She also writes plays and scripts for All India Radio. Her plays have won prizes in the prestigious Sultan Padamese Playwriting Competitions. In 1979 her radio play Brides Are Not For Burning *won BBC's first worldwide playwriting competition. Her delightful "Absolution" appeared in* SSI *No. 30.*

"It was empty of humanity, filled only with boredom."

Snow in Paris

BY SITOR SITUMORANG

HE threw the blankets back as though he had not slept at all.
Outside the city was covered with snow. Its whiteness pressed into
the dark room. He stood and his feet searched on the floor for his
slippers. The floor was as cold as ice. Downstairs he could hear
Madame Bonnet calling Monique.

He turned to the window. The snow fell before his half-awake
eyes like scratches on a film. It was very cold and very quiet.

Standing in front of the washbasin he unthinkingly turned on the
hot tap. The water burnt his hand. He withdrew it angrily and
turned on the cold tap. The sound of hot and cold water splashing
together in the basin warmed his blood a little. It was a very cold
winter. He went and took his coat from the hook behind the door.
Powder fell from the folds of the coat.

He dragged himself back to the basin. It was empty. He had
forgotten to put the plug in. There were a few long strands of hair
in the basin.

He went back to sleep.

When he looked at his watch again it was eleven. Monique had knocked at his door some time ago. The bellows roared in Room 15, next to his.

He sat down again, hoping that Monique would come in. Monique knew everything and said nothing. Madame Bonnet knew too, but she was different. She was a widow and understood because of her own experiences. Monique understood intuitively. Her eyes were soft, she smiled, and she did the work expected of her.

In the mornings she looked after Madame Bonnet's three children and dressed them for parish school. She opened the door for André, the bar attendant, a retired chauffeur. She dusted the furniture. Then she woke the boarders. The daily sound of her shoes on the stairs at a certain time was one of those important, unnoticed sounds of morning, like the plumbing.

He decided that she was not coming and, surprisingly, this cheered him. He began to whistle. The bellows stopped for a moment and then started again, more loudly than before. He forgot Monique and went downstairs.

"Bonjour monsieur André, bonjour Madame!"

Did they reply or not? André placed a thick cup of coffee, ground coffee as he always stressed, in front of him. He had learnt that the Indonesian did not like coffee essence.

The customers came in. Almost all of them were drivers from the large service station under the nearby building. They brought the wind with them. They rubbed their cold hands together, then stamped their dirty boots on the threshold trying to shake off some of the mud and dirty snow. Then, slowly, the door clicked back on its spring again. "Bonjour!" Then they climbed onto the round bar stools.

André served them wine and coffee. Some ordered wine and ate their own bread. Already big men, their size was magnified by their thick, dirty jackets. He saw them in relationship to André and his bar. He watched the skill with which André poured and mixed his drinks. Every day. He wondered if any other day was any different. Behind André's large square head stood colored bottles of wine with various labels. Cinzano, Dubonnet, and so on. The men said very little. Their very presence was part of a pious morning silence.

The room was calm like a village restaurant.

"Will you have lunch here, monsieur, or shall I wrap some sandwiches for you?"

He shook his head, almost like a spoiled child, and walked to the door. The door swung noisily back and closed behind him. The snow enfolded him and was as cold as ice. For a moment he was startled.

Right or left to the center of the city? The falling snow stabbed at his hair and ears.

They had met a few days ago. It was later in the day than this, but snowing in exactly the same way. Five days ago? Yes. Today was Monday. Last Thursday.

He had gone to police headquarters, the Prefecture, to renew his alien's residence permit. It was something he had to do at certain periods. Because he had lived fifteen years in Paris, once a year was sufficient. It was easy for an artist to get a permit. *Peintre*, artist, he wrote, although he had painted nothing for the last five years. He wanted to be a poet too. Paris invited him to be a poet with its various moods, to express himself, but he had never been able to. Once. Five days ago, on the first night with the girl. They sat on the terrace of a restaurant by the Seine, facing Notre Dame's white soaring spires in the snow and lamplight. "A prayer raised to God," he had said. She wrote it down in the small red notebook she carried in her bag. He was sorry then. Ashamed of himself. But he said nothing. Had they really met and spent four nights together?

After he left the Prefecture he had felt an anxiety similar to that he once felt leaving the Marche aux Fleurs, the flower market. He saw a person, a woman, through the snow. She approached him and stood nervously in front of him. For a moment their eyes met.

He could not explain why, but her eyes seemed to detect his anxiety and he turned quickly to buy a paper from the lame man. Years later, as though in a dream, the snow of memory formed an almost incomprehensible barrier which separated him from the millions in the city and bound him in the same space as herself. Everything else seemed external to them. He looked at the leaden coin in his hand. It was real.

Was she speaking to him? "Monsieur, do you speak English?"

Momentarily he was startled and wondered how long it had been since someone spoke to him. "Yes."

The girl—she was still young—explained her problem. She wanted to go to Switzerland. She had come from London and now wanted to travel on. But she had no photograph for her visa and needed one because she was an Asian.

"Suivez-moi," he said reassuringly, with a wave of his hand. Unconsciously he was talking French, but she understood and followed. There was an island in the middle of the Seine where one could get photographs "in ten minutes." They walked beside Notre Dame, turned left into a lane and through a narrow door to the small photography chambers under the sign "HERE for your passport photographs" and a pointing hand.

Inside she took off her overcoat. She was slender and attractive. Her suit was wine-red. He stood in the corner like a tourist guide and watched her comb her hair.

As she posed, he looked at her more carefully from the side: her face, hair, breasts, hands and feet. The impression was inconclusive. She was pretty. Was she married? How old was she? She had both a child's simplicity and a woman's firmness. Two photographs. Now they had to wait. Their eyes met and he looked elsewhere.

"I'd like to use the phone. Can you help me, please? The French directory is so different from the English."

"What number do you want?"

"I don't know. Hotel Empire."

There were six Hotel Empires. He asked which road it was on. She didn't know.

"What is it near?"

"Saint Lazaire station."

He recognized one, or at least thought that he did.

"Whom would you like to talk to?" he asked, covering the mouthpiece with his hand.

"Mr. Stone, Room 115."

He hid his surprise. Even more surprising: "Mr. Stone has checked out and left." The girl showed no emotion. They paid for the pictures and left in silence. They walked close together, perhaps because of the cold, seeming to understand each other implicitly, like old friends.

In the police station he learned that her name was Margareth Roderigo.

"I'm Machmud."

She looked at him for a moment. "Are you Indonesian?"

"Yes."

"I'm Filipino."

They walked aimlessly through the falling snow.

"Do you still want to go to Switzerland?"

"No."

He understood. "Come and have a drink."

That was all. Five days ago. That night he took her back to the hotel. They met Madame Bonnet on the stairs. He didn't introduce the girl. Madame smiled at them. "Pretty," she said to no one in particular as she descended the stairs.

Margareth was beautiful. She accepted the warmth he gave her like an elegant cat stretched before a fire.

Bonnet's "family" accepted the situation. Madame made no comment. Monique called Margareth "madame": he hoped that she at least would ask how and why. It was all quite informal. "Madame" seemed to be Margareth's by right. She went everywhere with him in those few days. She met the friends he borrowed money from and went to the embassy where he worked half-days writing stencils for other ministries and embassies to throw away.

No one asked about her.

He wanted them to. He wanted to ask her things himself.

He wanted Aimée, the Jewish girl, to ask how and why he had disappeared. Aimée was nice but hard as iron. She wore long sleeves to cover the numbers tattooed under her fine skin in Buchenwald. He wanted them to ask him about love, faithfulness, betrayal and friendship. But they didn't. He had long ago given up asking about such things.

He wanted to ask Margareth, but in her silence she seemed to feel no need for questions. He couldn't pretend she did. She lived in a dream and he wanted her out of there. Free. But she said nothing. Neither did he.

All night he wanted to ask about her and tell her about himself.

Because it was cold and Margareth was still asleep, he left for work on his own. He wanted to be alone.

As he descended the stairs he met Monique. "Is madame awake?"

"Not yet. Wake her at eleven. You can take her coffee now, please. Er...and tell her that I will be back at six."

When he went into a restaurant near the Metro for a drink, he met Wong. It was close to six. He was annoyed. He disliked Wong, especially at that moment. Old Wong was like himself, although his parents were Indonesian Chinese.

Wong had lived in Paris for twenty years. He had taken his French wife back to Indonesia after he graduated from the Sorbonne, perhaps before, and they had lived in Jakarta for two years. Wong had come back and spent twenty years looking for her. That was the story at least. Whether it was true or not, nobody knew, just as no one knew whether he had ever found her, or even what he did for a living.

Although Machmud couldn't say why, Wong's life seemed to be his own. Despite the fact that he had never married, they were similar. There was no doubt about that. He had never tried to work out why. He only knew that he disliked meeting Wong. Not because of his bald head or his glasses, or the wrinkles around his mouth, not even because of the sad, patient and mischievous look in his eyes. He often felt sorry for Wong, especially when Wong cadged coffee from him.

Wong stood in front of the cashier, with his back to the door, buying his sweepstake ticket. Machmud tried to leave but Wong turned and saw him through the cigarette smoke and the haze of muffled voices. He endured Wong's dreams of what he would do with the fortune he was going to win from the horses.

At ten he arrived home. He met no one downstairs. André was at the back of the bar. His heart beat fiercely as he ran up the stairs. He knew. It wasn't just imagination.

The room was clean and moistly warm. It was empty of

humanity, filled only with boredom. Cleaned, slept in, cleaned, slept in. It never spoke, never asked any questions, and no one asked anything of it. Monique looked away.

He went downstairs. André was there, arranging the bottles on the shelves. Madame did not come out. Everything stopped and revolved around his loneliness as he sat and stared at the marble table.

That was last night. He had gone out and walked in the snow. He passed a bus.

The snow lay thick on the path and the roots. He walked, then stopped and looked around at his footprints in the snow. A few pigeons flew around looking for food.

The falling snow gradually filled his footprints, covered the mud, and returned everything to white. As white as the empty road ahead of him.

Sitor Situmorang's story shows the influence of his two years in Paris in the early 1950's. Primarily known as a poet, his stories are short and simple. He works with themes familiar in his poetry: alienation, disappointed love and the search for greater self-understanding. Harry Aveling, a noted translator of modern Indonesian and Malay literature, translated this story.

"The Arab was amazed at the question,
but he hastened to answer."

Crumbs

BY AMNON SHAMOSH

IN Aram Zova, in Aleppo, they tell a tale about Hakham Ezra
Hamawi of blessed memory, concerning a deed which exalted him
in the eyes of the gentiles and won him a name in all the cities of
the East. This happened years and years ago, but old and young
still tell it and bless the Lord who gave His wisdom to human flesh
and blood.

And this is the way the tale is told: A Muslim Arab, one of the
notables of the city of Aram Zova, returned home one night drunk
as Lot, may it never happen to you. He entered noisily and called
to his wife to make him coffee. "And hurry up *ya mara* (O
woman)!" he shouted, pounding his fist on the table. In his right
hand, the man held a half-eaten cake. Waving the cake around, he
said to his astonished wife, "If the coffee isn't ready by the time I
eat all this cake, you'll be divorced from me." Three times he
repeated these last words. As everybody knows, a Muslim who says
to his wife, "You're divorced," is considered as giving her a divorce
decree and can't take it back.

The poor woman hurried and, with trembling hands, stirred up the coals and put water into a brass coffeepot. But, before the water boiled, her husband finished the cake, rubbed his hands together and said to her, "Go back to your father's house, *ya mara.*"

The next day, the man opened his eyes and, as from a nightmare, what he had done rose up before him. After he had washed away the traces of the wine and sleep had left him, he began to repent. First, he loved his wife very much. Second, the act would bring disgrace on him and detract from his honor and position. And worst of all, his wife was from a good family, her father was one of the pillars of the exchange market and his revenge would be great. Therefore, the Arab ordered his carriage readied and went with a heavy heart to the great Kadi, he who is the highest judge of the Muslims.

With choked throat and tearful eyes, he told his story.

"One crime leads to another, *ya effendi,*" the Kadi said. "If you hadn't got drunk, you wouldn't have made the biggest mistake of your life."

The man agreed that he had sinned and begged the judge, "Please have pity on my honor and save my house."

The Kadi replied, "What's done cannot be undone. That's the judgment of the Koran."

"My life is in your hands," the man declared.

"I don't see any way out," the Kadi told him. "But if there's no hope left, come with me to the Dayan, the wise man of the Jews. He's a learned and clever man, a hot pepper. Possibly he'll find a scheme."

Hakham Ezra Hamawi was the Dayan, head of the court of the Jewish community in Aram Zova in those days. He opened his gates and his ears to the two Arabs and after he heard what he heard, he shut his eyes and put his hand on them, like someone saying the "Shema"—and the stillness all around was as deep as the sea.

After a short time, the Hakham shook himself, stroked his beard and asked, "Was the cake fresh or hard?"

The Arab was amazed at the question, but he hastened to answer. "Indeed, the cake was hard. A big *ma'moul* that I brought with me from the tavern."

"So," the Dayan advised, "get into your carriage and go to your father-in-law's house and call your wife to return home to you. She's not divorced and she's not banished from your house."

The Arab started to say, "But, according to our decree..." and peeked at the Kadi.

Then the Dayan advised, "According to the laws of your faith, she's still yours, *ya sheikh,* and your house is her house."

The Arab fell at his feet and kissed them. The Kadi asked in a whisper, "But how did you arrive at that decision?"

The Dayan said to the Arab, "Please repeat to the Kadi, may his glory be great, what you said to your wife last night."

The Arab repeated, "If the coffee isn't ready by the time I eat all this cake, you'll be divorced from me, divorced from me, divorced from me."

Said the Dayan, "Here's the matter. The woman will come home and make you coffee, as usual. And you—after you drink the coffee, get down on your knees and gather up the crumbs of the dry cake from the rug. Only after all the crumbs have come into your mouth, and your gullet, will all the cake be eaten."

The Kadi shook his head and said, "Your judgment is a real judgment, O Hakham. And I'll put my seal on it."

The Dayan answered, "There's no dry cake without crumbs and there's no problem without a solution."

And all the Arabs of the city, Muslims and Christians alike, who heard how Hakham of the Jews had saved an honored family from shame and disunion, whispered to one another, "Blessed is the generation that was worthy of a Dayan like that and happy is the nation that has the likes of him."

Amnon Shamosh is one of Israel's most prolific writers and a prominent figure in the new wave of writers from Oriental countries. He has won the Prime Minister's Award for Creativity and the Jerusalem Agnon Prize for Literature. Mr. Shamosh was born in Syria in 1929 and arrived in Israel in 1938. He is a founding member of Kibbutz Maayan-Baruk. Barbara Benavie translated this story.

"I said something perfectly foolish and then climbed the tree feeling something of a hero and an ass."

The Folly

BY TARIQ RAHMAN

WHEN Talib Hussain, lecturer in Mathematics at the Boys' Degree College in town, moved into the yellow stone house, he was greeted by a middle-aged man with a bald pate and a constipated smile on his face. The man introduced himself as Dr. Aslam Bhatti and offered Mr. Talib Hussain his hospitality for the evening. In the evening, a meal came from the doctor's house and the Hussain children, much to their mother's satisfaction, ate it with relish.

"Nice decent man, this Doctor Sahib," said Mrs. Hussain.

Her husband grunted. He was chewing a bone and considered talking something of a trial when eating, but his wife insisted on talking all the time.

"You must visit his wife," he said after he had finished and had lighted a cigarette.

"Yes, tomorrow," she said eagerly.

The men met later in the evening and Dr. Bhatti took his new neighbor for a stroll.

"What's that huge building?" asked Talib Hussain, pointing towards some architectural ruins stretching over a vast piece of land.

"Oh, that. That's a long story, Professor Sahib."

Talib Hussain, much gratified at being called *Professor*, though most people called him that, maintained an expectant silence for some time. His companion's enigmatic smile became a shade more enigmatic and he said that the ways of God were strange.

"The ways of the Almighty are strange," concurred Talib Hussain enthusiastically, and waited for the story to begin.

The sun started setting and as it sank into the green fields, it touched the conglomeration of tall buildings at several points. Dr. Aslam Bhatti stood watching with a faraway look in his eyes. "This is the story of the days when I was a mere boy," he said in a theatrical tone.

Talib Hussain's face manifested signs of deep interest, for his curiosity had been whetted.

"But, really, I will tell it to you some other day," said the doctor hurriedly. "I said I would attend some patients. When they call me to their homes, I take not less than fifty."

Talib felt disappointed till he remembered that he had given an appointment to some students who wanted him to tutor them, and he needed to make preparations. He would not take less than two hundred rupees for the month.

"Some other time then, Dr. Sahib," he said with good grace, and they parted.

The students came rather late the next day but he let them go early and asked them to bring along some other weak students. Then, as he was preparing to go out for a walk, Dr. Bhatti knocked at his gate.

"Welcome," he said, opening the gate. "Won't you come in?"

"I was going for my customary walk."

"I, too, was thinking of doing that."

"Well," enthused the doctor, "let's go then."

They talked about their professional lives. The doctor said he worked nine hours a day. Talib, in turn, told him that he taught three hours after college. Then they saw the ruined house and Talib, egged on by reawakened curiosity, reminded his companion of the story of the house he had started telling. "It looks like a haunted house," he added by way of instigating his companion to talk about it.

The doctor looked at the house with a blend of nostalgia and melancholy. "I have memories attached to that house," he said with studied softness.

Again, Talib waited and again, the doctor confined himself to shakes of the head, rolling of the eyes and mysterious exaggeratedly sibilant sighs.

"Some tragedy," suggested Talib sympathetically.

"One could say so," said the doctor mysteriously.

They had walked back to the doctor's house. The doctor paused and pointing his cane at the setting sun said histrionically, "The days of the great are over. The great are great in everything, even in their follies. What you see, Professor Sahib, is the folly of the great!" And then, as if overcome by nostalgia, he said sentimentally, "Please come in and I will tell you the story of the house."

They entered without a word. Dr. Bhatti had Talib sit in a wicker chair, positioned so he could see the house silhouetted against the twilight. Tea arrived and they lit cigarettes and settled down.

"When I was a child of eight," began the doctor, "this town was little more than a village. There was only one primary school and no hospital at all. There was only one family that owned a proper brick and cement house with whitewashed rooms. This was the family of Daulat Baig. The Baig Sahib had been given all the land you see around you by the Mughals. He was rich and was the first one to buy a car. When the car arrived we children couldn't believe our eyes. It was wonderful and a little frightening to see this strange thing move without horses. And it went so fast and churned out such clouds of dust that we never could believe it was made by man."

"Which car was it?" asked Mr. Hussain, who always wanted to know unimportant details.

"I don't know. It was a big, black car," replied the doctor with a touch of acerbity. He loved telling stories and resented interruption.

Talib Hussain, who had become fascinated by the melodious, well-regulated voice of the narrator, was sorry that he had interrupted. "Go on, Dr. Sahib. Go on, please," he pleaded.

The doctor resumed. "As I was saying, there was this car. And in the car sometimes we saw a little girl. Like a little angel she sat there. And she always looked out with eyes which didn't see us—the boys who ran chasing the dust clouds."

"Sahib, a man insists on seeing you," interrupted Dr. Bhatti's servant.

His voice jarred Talib Hussain and his host, too, seemed annoyed.

"Who is it?" he asked crossly.

"The fat Chaudhry Sahib's servant. He says Chaudhry Sahib is ill."

"Oh," said Dr. Bhatti, jumping up from his seat, "I'll be there in a moment."

"Chaudhry Sahib," said the servant by way of apology as he led Talib Hussain out, "is so rich that he calls the doctor even when someone sneezes; he doesn't mind paying double fees."

Talib Hussain kept thinking of the sylph-like girl in the car. Perhaps, he thought, she was lying buried somewhere in the picturesque ruins of the house the doctor called "The Folly."

The men could not meet the next day nor the day after. Mr. Talib Hussain had added students to what was now almost a private coaching center. He worked about four hours after college. His colleagues joked that during college hours he didn't work even one hour. The doctor, too, was busier than ever. But autumn evenings were resplendent in that semi-rural area and Talib Hussain found himself intrigued more than ever by the house with which legends were associated. One day he found the doctor already there. They shook hands warmly and without preliminaries the doctor began:

"Where was I? Oh yes, chasing that angelic little girl. It was autumn as it is now and crops were being harvested. There was color all around and the leaves were falling. On one such day I saw her all alone reading a book near the place where we are sitting now."

"Was this culvert there then?" Talib Hussain could not resist asking.

"No; there was a huge stone here. She was sitting on it. The book in her hand had butterflies on the cover. I stopped here—there were bushes of roses here—and pirouetted on my heels. I didn't know how to talk to her. I stood still like an egret till she lifted her eyes and looked at me. They were beautiful hazel eyes and so fascinating that I felt myself drawn to her as if she were a magnet and I an iron nail. Then she got up and, with light steps, walked away. The book was in a language I didn't understand."

"English," said Mr. Talib Hussain helpfully.

"French," replied the doctor, stung to the quick.

For some time there was silence. The sun had set and the building looked like a huge whale, and all around it were black shapes: a school of whales.

"It is rather late now. Shall we postpone the rest for another evening?"

"If it suits you better," agreed Talib reluctantly.

They met off and on but the examinations were near and Mr. Talib Hussain was working five hours in the evening. He had a whole school to teach and his wife had more *saris* then she could wear. But still he wanted more students. Doctor Bhatti was busy, too. His practice had increased and he had become the physician of the affluent class. He, too, had more money than he ever had before. So it was winter when the doctor himself came to his neighbor's house in the evening. The friends had tea and lit their cigarettes.

"What happened in the story?" asked Mr. Talib impatiently.

"Well," said the doctor, inhaling with pleasure, "we discovered that her name was Shaista. The boys with me were all a bit shy of her. She rendered them speechless. It wasn't her beauty alone. It was an ethereal quality she had. She was so graceful, even as a little girl. Her features were delicate and she was fair. Her brown hair cascaded down to her shoulders and she had a strange quality of not being of this world. I started talking about her to one of my friends and, in order to maintain secrecy, gave her the code name of "Brown Buffalo.""

"Brown Buffalo!" burst out Mr. Talib.

"Brown Buffalo," said the doctor a little wistfully. "Yes, I know it was not apt. But that's why we chose it—to throw people off the scent.

"Well, Shaista was to be seen only during the holidays. She

studied in a school run by English nuns—or possibly Irish ones—in the hills. But when she came to the town the very atmosphere changed: things seemed more fresh, more colorful and there was excitement and magic in the evenings. The boys cycled around the brick house, and when the black car came out of the drive, cycled onto the grass on the sides and rolled off their cycles laughing.

"I was about fifteen and Shaista fourteen when Daulat Baig died, leaving his immense estate to his widow and two children: Shaista and Ikram Baig. Ikram, a sickly child of eight, was not at home but Shaista was. Of course, she didn't reveal her sorrow to me. In fact, I never saw her. She went away to the hills in August.

"Soon after we saw much activity in this area"—the doctor waved his arm vaguely in the direction of The Folly—and wondered what Begum Baig was up to. Trucks of cement arrived, bricks were unloaded at night and people went about taking measurements and looking busy. We boys talked of nothing but the new developments and went riding in the trucks to the brick-kilns. The laborers, rather uncouth young men, told us that a big house would be constructed. It would have so many rooms that no one person could remember them all, one of them said with a wink. Another one, carried away by the spirit of exaggeration, told us that it would have dungeons and mazes where boys could lose their way and never get free rides again. Some of us told them that they were fools and that no houses could ever be like that.

"'There's a law against that,' shouted my friend Asalm.

"'It's against the rules of geometry,' rejoined Gulzar.

"'It's against the rules of probability,' I added.

"The laborers were impressed. They had never imagined we knew those big words and now that we had sprung the words on them, they were dumbfounded.

"'It's for a big house,' concluded one of them lamely, going hastily to join his companions.

"The foundation of the house was dug. Then a man arrived in a white car. It was rumored he was a great architect from the city. This man wore a suit and a hat and walked as if he hated the dust under his feet. He screwed up his nose every now and then and looked offended with everybody. The chief mason approached him, salaamed low, and started telling him something about the house. The man looked even more offended. In fact, whenever someone spoke the architect winced as if in pain. And then *he* started speaking, and he spoke for no less than an hour. He didn't look at anyone in particular but spoke as if no one were present. After that, men dug the earth like mad. This went on for a year.

"In the winter holidays Shaista came again. She wore English dresses and I found her so beautiful that I would not dare look at her. And she read French books and talked to her friend, an English girl, in fluent English. Her horse—did I tell you she had a horse which she rode sometimes?"

"No."

"Well, she did. And this horse had been sold. Begum Baig said she wanted the stables to turn into something useful. So Shaista didn't ride and she had nothing to do. One day my kite fell onto their property. I would have let it lie there but Gulzar dared me to get it. I told him about the dogs but he reminded me that the kennels had been demolished and all they had were pet poodles.

"'You aren't afraid of those clowns on four feet?' he taunted me.

"'No, I'm not,' I replied defiantly.

"I marched in without apparent hesitation. There were so many people about that nobody noticed me. But I had to go towards the little garden around which was a thick green hedge. I slipped in and found my kite. As I was going to return I heard the rustling of clothes. And there she was. I stood petrified. Then I held my kite up and showed it to her.

"'Please take it,' she said with a smile.

"She went out and I stood there for a short while lost in the sweetness of her voice. Then, with numb feet, I came out and showed the kite to my eager friends. But Gulzar had watched my encounter with her from the top of the highest tree, and I couldn't deny having talked to her. They asked me so many questions that I ran away, refusing to admit them into that private world. And that night a new warmth made me turn and toss in bed. Again and again I closed my ears to the sounds of the night, the chirping of crickets, the cries of the watchman, and tried to hear her voice.

"The foundation had been dug. An army of donkeys filled the

hollows with the earth; another army brought stones, concrete and cement. The laborers worked and laughed in the shade of trees. The foundation was coming up. Then other men drove up from the city and work was stopped. For months men ran here and there and everybody shouted at everybody else. Then some of the foundation was torn down and a new section built.

"When Shaista came back, her younger brother, still a puny child, was with her. The two went out for long walks in the evening. This was, of course, unconventional but no one expected Shaista to go into *purdah* or wear *burqa*, so no one thought this strange. She was more beautiful than the actresses in English films and now that she was sixteen some people said it was dangerous for her to go about unchaperoned. But for us, for me, it was a blessing that I could still see her, although there could be no opportunity of meeting her. Not even while fetching kites. We looked down when she approached though my heart beat wildly and I couldn't even look my friends in the eyes later.

"But one day, that winter, I did see her closely. Her brother had taken her to their orange orchard. It was being cut down because their mother wanted more land for the house. The brother and sister were sorry that the orchard would have to go the way of the stables and the kennels. The day Ikram took her there, he climbed a tree himself. But he was not a good climber and couldn't reach out for the best oranges. Every time he tried he hurt himself. I was going hurriedly by, my eyes lowered, when Ikram slipped and hung precariously from the branch. I ran and caught him in my arms. She had jumped forward impulsively and when I put him down she murmured her thanks. I said something perfectly foolish and then climbed the tree feeling something of a hero and an ass. I reached out for the best oranges and threw them down. She didn't catch them in the air but her face beamed with joy when she bent down to gather them. Ikram recovered so far as to catch them in the air with shouts of glee. Then I came down and started walking away. Ikram ran after me and thanking me shyly gave me two of the very best oranges.

"'No,' I protested, 'I don't want them.'

"'Sister says you should have them,' he insisted.

"I took them. I held them close to my heart and went slinking through the trees to be alone with my thoughts. A great flood of tenderness surged into me and I caressed the oranges. I went home and lay moodily in the yellow and brown grass. And when I went out in the evening the crisscross maze of the foundation of Mrs. Baig's house seemed alien in the lawns of the green and red house where Shaista lived.

"She went away and I started studying hard. Not to make myself worthy of her like the boys in the films, but only because I wanted to rise above the boys whom she had not honored. I never once thought of marrying her. And other thoughts, unmentionable ones which I couldn't drive away, goaded me into acts of desperation: running six miles on winter mornings, cold baths, and—the idiocies of adolescence.

"Meanwhile the walls of the house grew up like a calf. The trouble was that people came to knock down the walls and build better ones; thus new ones were always being built. But for this the house would have been completed. But it wasn't completed. The laborers put in improvised sheds and then built huts. A hotel started running in a thatched hut and small boys scurried hither and thither like ants. They had kettles of tea in their hands, plates of food on their heads and words for everybody they served. I went to the city to enter college and came home during the holidays.

"The house was not completed but it looked like a castle now. The façade was improving and one could see an impressive array of windows from the street. But Begum Baig, said my friends, had borrowed more money to put marble on the floors. Slabs of marble arrived when I was still in the town. Other outlandish things also arrived and sophisticated decorators came to decorate the house. Then Begum Baig decided to add another room and that work started again. Shaista was nowhere to be seen.

"I did well in my F.Sc. and went to the Medical College. In the summer I stayed in the hostel and worked hard..."

Someone knocked on the door. Mr. Talib got up reluctantly and opened the door. It was a youth whom he was supposed to tutor. Mr. Talib had asked him to come after the evening meal and the boy was apologetic fearing he was late.

"Tomorrow," said Mr. Talib.

The boy brightened visibly and left immediately.

"I hope my patients don't come knocking here," mumbled the doctor. His practice was so big that the Bank Manager joked that his bank would be robbed only because of the doctor's cash.

"I do hope no one needs you," said Mr. Talib and settled down in his chair.

"As I was saying," began the doctor, "I didn't go home till the winter. That was when Shaista generally came home, but she wasn't there. Her brother was but, of course, I didn't talk to him about her. He did seek me out once or twice and talked to me. He was rather anaemic and frail-looking but pleasant to talk to. He told me that another room was being added to the left wing. It would be a sun-room and the walls would be of glass. Someone else told me that the whole façade would be overlaid with white marble. Begum Baig had sold off all her land and the money, hundreds of thousands of rupees, would be spent on the house. The main hall would have running water in it and three fountains would decorate the house. My friend Gulzar, the local apothecary now, told me that Shaista was a student of Fine Arts in Paris. Her paintings were being exhibited in Europe and she was making a name for herself. We both felt a bit overawed and then slipped back into the local habit of discussing the house. We agreed it would be a marvel like the Taj Mahal; some people joined in and said that the house would be like the Red Fort of Delhi. This was hotly disputed and we left them arguing about it.

"When I came back again for the following holidays, there was a sense of urgency in the town. The house was like a palace but the whole left wing was now of red-hued stone. And new rooms were being added. These rooms were being completed in great haste, laborers working night and day. A canal had been dug to supply running water. However, it was rumored Begum Baig had sold everything which belonged to her, and her son was not to be sent to England for higher studies. The car was still there but it hadn't been changed. Shaista was still abroad.

"Then, when I was back in the city, a letter came from home giving me a bombshell of news: Shaista had been called home. Her mother could not afford to have her stay in France any longer.

"When I next returned home, Begum Baig had started building a summerhouse, too. This building would be of black granite—a most unsuitable color for summer in my opinion—and would be connected to the main house by a bridge. I didn't see any sense in the bridge but I was assured there would be a bridge. Shaista was at home but was not to be seen anywhere. She was buried somewhere in the completed left wing, the huge structure of red stone which one can still see from the road.

"It was my fourth year and the house was still not completed. Begum Baig wanted more rooms to be added. She wanted some airy rooms at the top. The bridge was left incomplete and these rooms were begun.

"Strange rumors started floating: that the land itself was mortgaged, that the house could not be completed because the Begum was bankrupt, that the immensely rich Seth Sahib who had advanced the money to Begum Baig was now pressing for payment. Then, one day Gulzar told me that the Seth had asked for Shaista's hand in marriage.

"'Shaista,' I shouted. 'But Seth Sahib is at least sixty.'

"'Well, not sixty, only fifty-seven,' said Gulzar mockingly.

"I was indignant. No! This couldn't be true. This was nonsense. But it wasn't nonsense. The incompleted house was decorated and Seth Bootwala arrived in a long white car. He was so fat that when he waddled out of the car, with beads of sweat rolling down his thick black neck, one child told another that he was a hippopotamus.

"I had been invited to the wedding dinner—perhaps because I was the only medical student in the town. Ikram, looking sad and pale and as anaemic as ever, welcomed me and asked me about college.

"'Why don't you take admission in the city,' I suggested casually. He winced and paled visibly. 'Perhaps I will,' he said evasively and laughed.

"People were discussing cement and water and decoration. This surprised me till I discovered that they were mostly connected with the building of the house. The Seth had brought only twelve people with him, seven of them ladies. The men were architects, engineers, plumbers, electricians and masons.

"Shaista's marriage was over but my pain did not subside. I felt she had been thrown away. I felt—not that she should have married me but that she should have been an artist. She would have decorated the world better then all her mother's architects were decorating her house, that house which was now an irregular collection of buildings in different styles, colors and fashions. There were straight Greek pillars next to Gothic intricacies; there were minarets and strange pagoda-like structures. And then there was the monstrous black fortress which went by the name of the summer house.

"I passed my M.B.B.S. and opened my clinic in this town. The house was still being built. I saw Ikram sometimes. He looked like a cadaver and went about as if afraid of getting caught. He was always running after contractors, arranging for stone, mortar, bricks and cement, and generally using all his energy to complete his mother's house. But his mother knew no satisfaction and the house swallowed up the gardens at the sides and encroached on the lawn. Out of both wings rooms and extensions jutted out.

"One evening I was sitting in my clinic when a man came running and told me that Begum Baig wanted my services. I took my things and went out expecting the car to be there.

"'You will have to sit on my cycle,' said the man apologetically. 'The car has been sold.'

"The corridors of the house were really like a maze, and they were ugly. Here and there the workmen had left their tools and iron lay rusting in heaps. Some laborers were busy polishing and ruling the floors of newly completed rooms. When I reached a carpeted room I heard sounds of someone shouting hysterically:

"'I am not mad, Mother. I am not mad!'

"The voice was Ikram's but I would never have believed that he could have such hysteria, such bitterness in his voice. Nor could I have believed that he could shout so loudly.

"A dignified woman with gray hair tightly plaited welcomed me with a hardly perceptible nod. Her thin, tightly-closed lips remained closed as she seated herself.

"'I will not be doped or drugged or sent to the madhouse,' shouted Ikram frantically. 'I am not to be buried in this tomb,' he shouted, waving his arms around and rolling his eyes grotesquely to the ceiling from which a chandelier hung. 'I will not be walled up alive in the walls of this house.'

"'My son is insane,' said Begum Baig distinctly and without a trace of emotion.

"'I will not marry the Seth's ugly daughter. She is deaf and dumb and fat and she is almost forty years old. She—she is my sister's daughter after all,' and he jumped up and hit the sofa so hard that he fell down himself.

"The man servant looked at his mistress but, since she remained impassive, just stood still. I thought I would prepare an injection of a tranquilizer in case Ikram—I was reluctant to call him the patient—got violent. And I was right. He got violent. He smashed things, especially the chandelier. Then he said he would burn the house and we had to overpower him, and I gave him an injection.

"But after two days he did set the house on fire. As the house was so spread out, only the completed wing was burnt. Ikram was sent to the psychiatric ward in the city hospital where the determination was that he could be kept at home. So he came back here and confined himself to one room. Everybody knew that the Seth had promised a dowry of two hundred thousand rupees if Begum Baig accepted his daughter as her son's bride. But now the Seth heard that the young man was mad and threatened to burn the house if this match was mentioned to him.

"When necessary, I was called to give Ikram injections of tranquilizers. I had forgotten what little psychiatry I had learnt but I thought he was manic-depressive. Sometimes he would sit in a corner and the tears trickled down his face while at other times he broke things in a fury and cursed the house to which rooms, shaped like cabins in a ship, were being added.

"'My sister is buried under the putrid, loathsome flesh of a huge buffalo,' he once told me. I felt the energy being drained out of my body. My throat was dry and I couldn't ask any questions. He didn't elaborate on this vituperative remark but added: 'I won't be sold. I won't be tethered to that hippopotamus.'

"Later, when I was away from the town. Ikram set fire to the house again. He himself perished in the fire while climbing up the stairs to destroy the new rooms. People said that he was getting better when his sister arrived. She was so miserable that Ikram started throwing things wildly and insisted on her going away with him. But Shaista had come to give all her jewelry, inherited from her grandmother, to her mother. Their mother was desperate for money: the workmen had to be paid, the incomplete rooms had to be finished. The jewelry was of solid gold ornaments studded with diamonds, and Begum Baig once again had enough cash to complete the house. But Ikram was dead.

"After that Begum Baig became a familiar sight. With a shawl wrapped around her, looking erect and severe, she stood under a huge tree. The workmen, obsequious under her eagle-like aristocratic eyes, walked around carrying heavy loads. They neither laughed, sang, nor shouted at each other. Human life, the hustle and bustle of it, seemed to cease where she was. But in the other parts of the house ribald jokes were told and people sang silly songs.

"Nobody knows how Shaista came to live with her mother again. There were all sorts of rumors afloat. Some people said her husband never forgave her for giving her jewelry to her mother. Others were positive that Begum Baig made her daughter demand her *maher* which was one lac rupees in cash. Still others said it involved a plot of land which Begum Baig had given to her daughter as dowry. The land was of no value when given but now it was of commercial use and of great value. The Begum wanted it but the Seth wouldn't part with it. I don't know what happened but Shaista was back and buried in one of the great empty rooms. Yes, the rooms were almost empty; their decorations had been sold so that a new room could be added.

Then I saw wonderful paintings in the bazaar. They were all signed by Shaista and to my eyes they appeared to be the greatest pieces of art of all times. I bought some—I'll show them to you."

"Not the one in which there is just one ripe apple on the tree and children are standing below looking at it?"

"Yes, that's one."

"What can it mean?"

"Mean? It's just a painting. It does not mean anything."

"Go on."

"The paintings sold very well and we heard she taught girls to paint, too. But she did that in the city where, it was rumored, she had to live in a single small room in a slum. Whenever she came home new paintings appeared in the bazaar. And the house was nearly finished! Even we, the outsiders, were relieved. The house had dominated the town for many years and there was an indefinable tension because of its incomplete state.

"One spring day I was called to the house again. They had only one servant, a mumbling old retainer, who couldn't ride a bicycle. But I had a cycle and reached the house as quickly as possible. This time there were signs of things being tidied up and finished. The walls were straight and looked massive and impregnable. The house looked more like a fortress than anything else, and it was bleak! The beautiful marble façade was no more, nor were there any signs of water, the canal and the fountains.

"I was feeling saddened but what shocked me beyond expression was the small dark room in which Shaista was lying. She seemed to be asleep but her mother, even more thin-lipped and severe than before, told me that Shaista was too weak to open her eyes. That was true because when I applied the stethoscope to her back she opened her eyes. They looked startlingly wide and dark against her pale, bloodless face. Her cheeks had hollows in them and blue veins stood out on her startlingly fair skin. She had fever and seemed completely exhausted. I suspected she had T.B.

"'She must have an X-ray taken of her chest, Begum Sahiba,' I told her mother. 'I think she has T.B.'

"The eyebrows of the Begun flickered and she looked at me intently. Then, without a word, she nodded and I knew I had been dismissed. She took out money for my fare.

"'I am a neighbor, Madam,' I said. 'This is not necessary.'

"'I don't like scenes,' she said distinctly and without kindness or even a perfunctory show of politeness. I took the money and went away.

"The X-ray report confirmed she had T.B., and in the third stage, too. It was no use sending her to a sanatorium. Still, I wanted her to get away from that atmosphere of urgency and insecurity. I told her mother it would be best to send her to the sanatorium. She was not sent there. I ventured to intrude once again. Shaista was resting against her pillows. She had been reading a book. I felt myself perspiring. She was like a mummy but still so beautiful.

"'Do you feel dizzy when you read,' I asked her, trying to sound professional.

"'I know this book much too well.'

"I wanted to ask which one it was but couldn't bring myself to do so. She must have guessed as much because she added, 'It's a French novel, *Le Pierre Goriot*...'

"Just then her mother entered and sat down stiffly. I prepared to leave my patient and asked Begum Baig if I could have a word with her. She seemed astounded at my liberty but followed me.

"'She is dying,' I said formally. 'The sanatorium may save her.'

"'I have asked the opinion of a specialist,' she replied sharply, 'and he says nothing will save her. It's no good moving her.'

"That was not entirely wrong and I had done my best to save her from the house where work was going on feverishly again. For just when the house might have been completed Begum Baig wanted another room, a library to be built. All the books, Shaista's books, had been sold a long time ago. But the library was to be built! I suspected Begum Baig didn't want to spare the money for the sanatorium.

"Shaista died before the summer rains started. I remember I was miserable and didn't eat, nor could I sleep that night. I know I was behaving like a sentimental idiot but I couldn't help it. It seemed unspeakably cruel that Shaista had died of T.B. in a desolate house where there was nobody to befriend her, and her mother was too busy supervising the construction.

"After Shaista's death, construction was speeded up. Walls were pulled down and rooms jutted out. The shape of the house was not even of a fortress any longer. It looked like a pile of gray, cement blocks with the new rooms piled on each other haphazardly. The façade itself disappeared and the architects were sent away. The engineers, too, had to go. Only the Begum remained and there was a team of unskilled laborers and an incompetent mason under her. And early every morning she stood rigid and straight, like a general, with a stick in her hand. When she spoke, it was with the hatred and the hissing of a wounded snake. But she supervised the mixing of concrete and cement, the lifting of bricks and stones and the making of the wall. In the afternoon she allowed the laborers to have their lunch; she, too, ate something. It wasn't cooked in her house any more but came from a shop. And she drank a glass of cold water and then, once again, in all kinds of weather, she stayed in her area of duty. Just before sunset she distributed the wages— for now there was no one to do it for her—and then tottered back to her bed. She no longer had any servants. Even the old retainer had gone home; he could hardly walk and his sons had not allowed him to go back. She was alone and the house was dark at night. She saved on electricity, people said, to pay for the building of a new room, yet another cancerous growth of what was once the beautifully decorated red left wing.

"This continued on and on! Like ants or bees or wasps which keep busy building their hives, Begum Baig went on building. Only a handful of laborers remained. Only one wall could be built but built it was. It rose inch by inch everyday, and in the evening she measured it and smiled with satisfaction. That tap-tap of her stick could be heard by those who trespassed in that huge haphazard mound of concrete and cement as I had, looking for the garden where my kite had fallen.

"One day she was declared bankrupt. There was no money to pay the laborers. The last one had departed and her goods had been sold to pay him. But she did not seem to mind. That evening when I was taking a walk I found her bustling about. Her body was a slave of her will and I couldn't believe my eyes when I saw her mixing cement with sand and actually putting a brick and plaster in place. She must have heard my movement because she turned around and gave me a look of withering animosity. I mumbled an apology and beat a hasty retreat.

"Then we heard that school children went and helped her with the building of a wall. For them it was a game, though they were intimidated by her grim silence, her peremptory tone and the gleam in her eyes. But they had great fun playing in the shade and carrying bricks where she could put them in the wall and fix them ever so carefully with cement.

"One day a number of children came running to inform us that the old Begum Sahiba had got buried under fallen bricks. We hurried to the house but it was too late. A roof had collapsed and she was buried under the debris. Nobody knew whether she had any relatives, so the neighbors buried her and prayers were said.

"The house was searched but all that was found were old, broken cooking pots, a plate, cups and saucers and one broken *charpoy*. There wasn't even a chair, and there were no ornaments nor books nor even clothes.

"Nobody claimed the house and nobody did anything about it. Years later a Baig relative turned up. We do not know what happened but the house is still lying incomplete—nobody knows what will be done with it. No one dwells in it. It is useless."

The doctor got up to go. The spell of the story broke and both men stared in the direction of the house, now enveloped by darkness and hidden from prying eyes. At the doorstep the doctor said:

"It's rather late. I must get some sleep to be fresh for work at the hospital."

"And I," said Mr. Talib, "for work at the college."

They shook hands and parted, both knowing that the other started work in earnest only after his regular work hours.

Born in 1951, Tariq Rahman served as a commissioned Army officer for eight years, resigning in 1978 to lecture at Karachi and Islamabad. A British Council award for further study at Sheffield University brought him to England, where he completed his PhD. Dr. Rahman now teaches at the university level in Pakistan. His publications include a volume of verse written in English, 40 short stories written in English, and articles on strategic studies, literary subjects and book reviews. He also translates stories by other writers from Urdu to English. His wife, daughter and son are a source of pride and comfort.

"What shall we do now?"

The Journey

BY CATHERINE LIM

RICHARD liked to tell his friends, "To me, to be able to sit for half an hour, just dreaming away, is a rare luxury," and he was having this rare luxury now, while waiting to be called into the consulting room. Richard leant back and sighed with pleasure. The satisfaction which a man feels when at the age of thirty-two, he has become the managing director of a large and established firm, commanding a salary that has enabled him to buy a large detached bungalow in one of the most prestigious housing estates in the country, two cars, one for himself and one for his children to be driven to school in by a chauffeur, a diamond ring for his wife that would cost a whole year's salary of some of his wife's working friends—this satisfaction cannot be merely called pleasure. It is pure bliss, and Richard felt it stir the depths of his soul. He was not one to be complacent about his good fortune; he was profoundly grateful for it and in this warm glow of gratitude, he thought of his mother, aunt and grandmother who had pooled whatever money they had to send him to school, and, later to college. Now he was repaying them ten-fold; he sent back a generous sum of money to them every month, and he told them in his letters, and on the few occasions when he saw them, "Leave that sleepy little village. Come to the city. Come and stay with me. You'll have all the comforts you've ever wanted. You'll have servants to cook for you. You can go shopping in the many shopping centers here. Get out of this backwater. Good Lord, it's such an *ulu* place that one will die of boredom and misery there. My dear grandma, mother and aunt, won't you come? There are three extra bedrooms in my house—and all air-conditioned too!"

They said no, politely. Grandmother said the air-conditioner was not good for her old bones. The last time she had come down for a holiday, she and Aunt suffered so much; Mother could bear things a little better. The three women had left in a hurry, and Mabel had sighed with relief. "It was such a trial with those three women in the house," she had confided to some of her friends at the office. "My mother-in-law slipped on the Italian marble floor in the bathroom and nearly injured herself. My grandmother-in-law has the obnoxious habit of chewing betel nut all the time and she once spat out the red juice in my patio. Would you believe it? I found a blob of that horrid stuff near my white cane chair. Oh, the horror of living with these people from the *ulu* places! Fortunately, it is not a permanent thing. My hubby asked them to come and stay with us more than once, but they weren't keen, because they're frightened of the air-conditioning. So we've done our part."

Women, sighed Richard, they were all like that, inclined to be too fussy and house-proud. Was Mabel house-proud! Richard's heart glowed in fond recollection of his wife's fine taste and artistry, evident everywhere in their beautiful bungalow, from the dark brown timbered ceiling, right down to the very table napkins. "The best, or nothing," Mabel said. She scoured the best shops, she bought the best things. When the boss and his wife came to dinner—the little coos of delight and admiration uttered by that charming, unassuming couple as they were shown round the house which they praised lavishly. Mrs. Harris was particularly taken by the Chinese antique table which Mabel had put in the corner of the hall. Mabel played down its price—"Oh, it costs a few hundred dollars," she had said casually when asked, but it had cost four thousand dollars; he had written a check for that amount when the delivery man came.

And now Richard's head became busy with mental arithmetic— *four thousand dollars*—Why, when he was a boy, living in that little village in that wooden house with a well near it and a thatched-roof latrine a few feet away—that sum would have represented two years' earnings to his mother, grandmother and aunt! His mother and aunt earned, if he remembered correctly, about a hundred dollars a month from their washing of clothes, his grandmother about fifty dollars from the sale of her cakes and puddings which the coffee-shop people came to collect every morning. Richard did some quick calculations: it would take the three of them more than two years to earn the sum which Mabel spent on this one antique, which, as Mabel was always pointing out, did not make her feel as guilty as the *other* antiques. "Put it down to my absurdity," she had laughed. But Richard thought fondly of the absurdity that had netted a clear ten thousand dollars; for Mabel had bought a quantity of antiques—pots, chests, chairs, tables—from a dealer in an obscure shop in a dark lane and sold all of them two weeks later for a cool profit of ten thousand. That ten thousand had been immediately converted into some shares which had soon afterwards risen in value. "It's Mabel's golden touch," Richard told his friends in an exuberance of spirits.

In celebration of the success, Mabel and he had gone shopping for things to decorate the house with, and for the children— Annabelle's piano (which was already three years old) was replaced by a brand new one, and Mark had a go-kart which pleased the boy no end.

His children—how fortunate, how absolutely lucky they were. They had all the toys and clothes which he and his sisters never had. "Toys, did you say?" Richard would pretend to explode in articulate incredulousness. "Toys? Never! You know what, we didn't even have proper food. I remember it was plain rice and some thin vegetable soup every day, or some cheap fish, that was all. No pork, no chicken, no eggs, except during the Chinese New Year. Nothing, except the cheapest food; at one time, we had plain rice and 'tau-foo' for days."

The girl Annabelle wanted to know what "tau-foo" was; Mark, abandoning the Lego set he was playing with, made ready to demand some "tau-foo."

Richard remembered the old wooden house well. He was born in it; he grew up in it. It was the very essence of filth and degradation.

The floor was beaten dirt; it was only years later that his mother had the cement laid. The furniture was old and rickety and bug-infested; the one mattress in the house was stuffed with coconut fiber, and was also bug-infested, and he remembered how he and his sisters had spent hours digging up the bugs hidden deep in the folds of the mattress, and killing them in a little saucer of kerosene. He never remembered himself and his sisters having proper towels, proper toilet soap, proper toilet paper. His aunt cut up old newspapers into little squares for the purpose. The latrine was one thing which, in his recollections, never failed to make him want to retch. It consisted of a raised wooden hut, four feet by two feet; the wooden floor had a round hole over which a person squatted directly over a waiting receptacle, an old rusty bucket. Once—he must have been eight or nine at the time—he had fallen through the hole, and his mother had taken a long time to clean him up, drawing up one bucket of water after another from the well. He had recounted this incident once to Mabel and had immediately regretted it, for she had felt quite ill and had forbidden him to talk of such things again. He remembered how he once fell ill—was that surprising, with the conditions as they were!—and how his mother, grandmother and aunt practically doused him in those horrible-looking, horrible-tasting herbal medicines that everyone in the village resorted to in times of illness. He remembered how, with his head bursting with fever, he tossed about on the hard coconut fiber-stuffed mattress, which was torn in some places so that the bristly fiber poked out and hurt his skin. There was no window in the room he was in; his mother had placed a chamber-pot near his bed for him to ease his bowels or vomit into, and he remembered the whole place stank and choked him. His aunt did a peculiar thing to cool his burning forehead; she cut up a potato into little thin pieces and spread them on his forehead, saying that that would take away the heat. Afterwards she showed him the blackened pieces, explaining that the blackness came from the fever which had transferred itself to the pieces of potato.

The superstitiousness of the three women was unimaginable; he wondered whether if his father were alive, conditions would have been more bearable. His grandmother was always prescribing strange cures for little sick children whose mothers came to her for help. Once a little girl was chased by dog, and fell ill the next day. The girl's mother came tearfully to Grandmother, and Grandmother got the girl's father to pluck out a bit of fur from the dog, and put it behind the girl's ear! He remembered that the parents carried the terrified child to their house, as she had resisted all their attempts to have the fur put behind her ear. But Grandmother took the child into her arms and touched and spoke to her so soothingly that at last she quieted down. Fur behind the ear of a frightened child! Mabel had been most amused, but she had cautioned him not to tell the children; they might develop superstitious or morbid notions.

He wondered how, with such an environment, he had managed to be where he was now. How culturally deprived had been his environment, how starved of the requisites of mental and emotional growth. Thank God Annabelle and Mark would never know such deprivation. He never had a toy; he remembered that the only toy he had had was a plastic bear with a broken nose which his mother had asked from someone for him, and he had treasured this toy and kept it hidden from his sisters.

One of his sisters had died. It was tetanus. She had stepped on a rusty nail, and his mother had applied some medicine, but three days later, she was dead. He remembered how grief-stricken his mother, grandmother and aunt were. The ignorance of those days! The women were convinced that an evil spirit had entered his sister's body and caused her death. Evil spirits, evil spirits—they were said to cause every illness and misfortune. How many deaths had been caused as a result of this belief! Richard felt grateful for the regular medical check-ups that he and his family were able to have. The nurse now appeared to summon him into the consulting room and he thought, Good. I shall be well in time for my golf. Shall pick up Mabel from the hairdresser's, and then drive on to a nice relaxing game.

He canceled the game. He took off his "Arrow" shirt and the Pierre Cardin tie that Mabel had given him for his last birthday, and sat down numbly on his bed. The children were clamoring, "Daddy! Daddy! Come and see our drawings!" but Mabel sent them out to play with the neighbor's children, and then quietly joined him in the room.

"What shall we do now?" he asked her in abject self-pity, and she burst into tears which became uncontrollable sobs. She sobbed miserably for a long time, and he continued to sit very still and gaze at the floral pattern of the brown-and-gold carpet on their bedroom floor. Mabel then sat upright and said that the doctor could be wrong—many doctors had been proved wrong in cases like this. But Richard told her the doctor in his case was positive; he gave him one year at most.

"I blame him," said Mabel bitterly. "You have been going to him regularly for the past four years, and how is it possible that he didn't detect it earlier? It seems impossibly irresponsible to me. And the fees he charges." She rang him up. She tried to keep her voice down, but it rose to a high pitch and finally Richard persuaded her to calm down.

"Richard," she sobbed again, "what's going to become of me and the children? Why didn't you give up smoking when I told you to?"

His mother, grandmother and aunt were told eventually, although Mabel had objected, saying, "We'll keep this to ourselves as far as possible. I don't want people hurrying over and pretending to feel sorry for us. The children must be protected from all this."

The three elderly women asked if they could come, and when Richard wrote back, "Please do. I want to see all of you again," they came. They avoided the sight of Mabel, and she, on her part, fretted. They brought along a certain herbal mixture which they said was good for him, but Mabel here put her foot down and said, "No. Richard's under the best medical treatment here. The doctors will not tolerate any traditional *ulu* cure."

Grandmother told her two daughters, privately, that she would have liked to spit in Mabel's face but had refrained from doing so, as it would have upset Richard. He was not in a condition to be upset. The three women stayed out of her way entirely; they ate separately, and Mabel took the children away to her sister's as frequently as she could. She appealed to her husband with tears in her eyes, "Darling, I'm not trying to be nasty to your folks, but it hurts me badly when I see them foisting their nonsense upon you, and you in this condition too. I want you to have none but the best; you deserve it, darling. Let me take care of you."

He had said wearily, "Mabel, leave them alone." He wanted to add, "They bring some comfort to me," but had remained silent after that.

They went home after some time, Grandmother embittered and angry, the two others silent and sad, and he felt a pang, but he let them go, and Mabel was less fretful.

He suffered. There was no pain as yet—but he suffered. He looked at his magnificent house (which a few days before a crew of men and women from the Television Department had arrived to film for a documentary which was to be called "Lovely Homes." Mabel had invited them over a month before, before they had learnt of the sad development). He looked at this lovely home of his, and he suffered keenly. Everything about him gave him pain, for he had worked so hard to get all these, and now they were dust and ashes in his mouth. He was still going to his office; he thought he might as well continue working, as sitting at home would be unbearable. Mabel had been consulting one specialist after another. One evening she came home with an excited look on her face and announced that she had found a specialist—the best cancer specialist in the world, based in New York. His chances of recovery under this specialist would be so very much increased. The expense would of course be enormous—but what was money? She was prepared to sell all the shares, her jewelry.

Richard said, "I'm a doomed man. I'm not going to make any journey to New York."

Mabel was sad. "It's no use," she told her sister. "I can't make him go to that specialist I told you about. I wonder what I can do to make him agree to make that journey?"

Richard dozed off a great deal. He thought of his boyhood in the small *ulu* village. He thought of the time when he was ill and lay on the prickly coconut fiber-stuffed mattress with the chamber pot nearby. He remembered how he had felt very ill and had wanted to vomit, but the stuff couldn't come out. He had agonized for a few minutes, making great retching noises in his throat, and he remembered his mother and aunt coming in. His mother's hands were still wet from her washing, and she wiped them quickly on her dress and came to him. She held him close and soothed his chest by rubbing it with slow gentle downward movements with her fingers. His aunt stood by, talking in low tones and then exclaiming happily when at last the vomit came out, and he lay back on the pillow, soothed. He remembered that his grandmother made him a brew, a black, bitter drink which she said was most effective when drunk in moonlight. He was sleeping when she gently picked him up from his bed and carried him outside, where the moonlight was streaming upon the house in a wonderful glow of warmth and peace, and she made sure his face was touched by the moonlight as he drank the brew. His grandmother tried to distract him from the bitterness by telling him a story about a moon goddess. He remembered it was a silly story, but it had the effect of calming him and allowing him to finish the brew.

In one of his dreams, Mabel was there as his grandmother carried him into the moonlight to drink his medicine. Mabel tried to snatch away the bowl of brew from her hands, shouting, "What nonsense! What nonsense!" Grandmother resisted, and in the ensuing struggle, the drink spilt all over him and stained him black. Mabel's face was hidden from him; in the darkness she continued screaming at them, and it was then that he woke up.

He told Mabel that he was going to make the journey for his recovery. He would go by train, and his mother, grandmother and aunt would meet him at the terminus and take him home. He was going home—When Mabel understood, she shrieked in agony. How can you be going back to that rotten little *ulu* village? Who will take care of you? What medical facilities could possibly exist there? How could she go to see him, with the business to see to and the children to take care of and the household affairs to manage? Mabel collapsed in tears, hurt beyond expression, struck to the depths of her soul. How could he think of such a thing? Was he sure that—Didn't he want to—

But he said, "I'm making the journey. I'm going home."

Catherine Lim writes short stories and teaches English literature at a junior college in Singapore. She is married and has two children. In reviewing her collection of stories, Austin Coates wrote: "She exposes men and women with a mixture of complacent ruthlessness and compassion." Her story "The Ugly One" appeared in SSI No. 65.

"There was nothing like a graceful 'loss of face' to ingratiate oneself with men like Stárov..."

The Hunt

BY JOSEPH PATRON

THEIR unmistakable presence at the Moser Hotel for British officers was a constant reminder of the encounter of East and West after World War II. They were the first Russians many Westerners saw on arrival in the British Zone of Occupation in Austria. The members of the Soviet Repatriation Mission were rarely seen alone, or even in couples. At the most, one of the four officers or the *N.C.O.* might be missing, perhaps through ill-health. The usual impression was of compactness, solidarity, uniformity, even drabness. They wore dark green uniforms, with the collar done up to the neck, above which peeped an inner white strip like an embryonic clergyman's dog collar. They were stocky in build and facially undistinguished. Their attention seemed always turned inwards, within their circle or else in the direction they were hurrying.

They led an isolated existence, occupying most of the top floor of the hotel, where only the hotel maids, or visitors from the Soviet Zone, could penetrate. Also, by using the back entrance of the hotel they could go in and out unobserved. As far as Lieutenant

Martin could tell—and as Liaison Officer and interpreter his contacts with them were frequent and close—they were monotonously regular in their habits. But he could see that living away from their own milieu was a strain on them. Their only form of relaxation was drinking at the hotel bar in the evenings, and perhaps later in their rooms. They received regular supplies of vodka from the Eastern Zone. Drinking, after all, is part of what it means to be a soldier, and especially a Russian soldier after a resounding victory. But they were obliged to abstain from relations with the local women, though as far as Martin knew they may also have made use of the back door of the hotel in the still hours of the night for this purpose. Most Austrian women felt it humiliating to be seen with members of the Forces of Occupation, though they made exceptions with the Western military; and for some reason they were altogether less choosy in Lower Austria, round the Klagenfurt area, where the Mission was centered. But the members of the Mission did on occasion disappear for weekends in the Soviet Zone; and they were visited for short periods by Red Army personnel from Vienna. Once one of the drivers (they had two) who had been drinking heavily, opened up with Martin about his love life, or the enforced absence of it because of their strict prohibition against fraternizing with Austrian *fraulein,* or for that matter, with any women in the hotel.

In the dining room the Mission had a Ukrainian waiter with whom they could communicate and who seemed always to be available. The peripheral position of their table made it possible for them to have their meals when they wished, in accordance with their flexible hours. They could, of course, converse with the locals in German: the limited conversational German they had picked up during their time in the German campaign. But Galánin, the N.C.O., who belonged to the Army Political Department (with the red band on the cap) was the only one who had studied the language and spoke it correctly. Colonel Savénko, the Head of the Mission, had only a smattering of German, though he did also speak French. Major Stárov, a rough, hard-drinking type—as Martin was later to discover to his cost—knew only a few phrases and words; but then, he was hardly articulate in his own tongue.

He had probably grown up, thought Martin, in the recently collectivized Soviet countryside. Lt. Col. Púnin spoke it well, and so did Lt. Spírin.

Hemmed in by these various barriers, they gravitated between their spacious quarters at the top of the hotel, their permanently reserved table at the far corner of the dining room, their excursions by car in search of displaced persons or refugees who might be willing to return to their country, and their evenings at the bar, or in one of the cubicles on the sides of the dance floor.

Sometimes they asked Martin to join them in the dining room, especially when they were preparing an excursion. It was as well, then, that their talk was muffled by the background music from the solitary Austrian pianist, for their conversation frequently wandered on to delicate ground. As Eisenhower and Marshall Zhukov were said to have done the year before in Berlin, they discussed the concept of freedom and its different practical applications. Fresh from his Cambridge Russian course, Martin had taken over only a few months before from the elderly Lt. Col. Rose who spoke Russian fluently, though with a marked accent; and Martin had read about the way political elections were conducted in the USSR. Sometimes, more through intellectual zeal than any polemical intention, he began a debate, especially with the more intellectual Savénko, who enjoyed prodding him—a mere upstart at twenty-one!—to get him to express his views openly. The others hung on every word, especially Galánin, with his bright blue eyes. It was usually in the interpretation that they differed, not in their view of the desirability of freedom in itself. One tricky question, for example, was the freedom of the press. Here they always talked at cross-purposes, for intelligent discussion of this topic presupposed a competence in social and political matters which neither side possessed. Of course, they were not aware that at this time the United Nations was drafting a document on human rights which treated precisely the subjects they discussed. When, later, Martin was posted to Vienna, after about a year "in the Zone," he had reason to suspect that Savénko may have been in some way instrumental in the transfer, perhaps by indirectly suggesting it. It may not have been wise, in the Colonel's view, for the less well-informed (or less ideologically formed) members of the Mission to be so often exposed to this kind of talk.

On the whole, the Mission members got to like their routine, though their cultural isolation weighed on them. When it did, they gathered for a drink in the evening, and Martin often joined them. Galánin was good at telling Russian fairy tales; it was his spare-time specialty. Once he got going, one could see he was the sharpest of the group, though in military rank he was the junior. Yet, he was not treated by the others as one of the rank-and-file. Their attitude to him was ambiguous: a mixture of respect and suspicion. Martin could not put his finger on what it was exactly that made him a foreign body in their midst. Once, a wise Ukrainian woman told him that among Russians politics acts like a poison, and that those who are not contaminated by it tend to avoid it and to cling together for protection. There was something of that, Martin felt, in the relations between N.C.O. Galánin and the officers in the Mission.

Moreover, it was Galánin who kept the accounts and took care of the correspondence. Here his knowledge of German was useful. Once, under the pretext of obtaining extra rations for a sick member of the Mission who was confined to his room, he arranged at a local dairy for a daily consignment of fresh butter and eggs (both strictly rationed commodities). Then the order was indefinitely prolonged even after the sick member was up and about. Since Martin had a share in the goods whenever he was asked to their table, and he was fully aware of the extreme need of the local Austrian population, he was an accomplice in the black-marketeering. This was, however, the aftermath of war; and in any case, would it have been better to refuse?

In the late evening get-togethers, and especially when they were seated tightly round the small table in one of the cubicles, entertained by the couples dancing to the small, lively orchestra, and with the connivance of vodka, Martin penetrated more deeply their impassive exterior, their massive reserve, to the whims and prejudices, the unsophisticated humor and the only partially indoctrinated minds; for except for Galánin, the military element was paramount in their lives.

Martin, as usual, addressed himself to Savénko—and also Púnin—not because they were senior, but because they were more talkative, though their talkativeness did depend hierarchically on their rank. Stárov concentrated on drinking; and Spírin hardly ever raised his voice, though he too drank heavily. One had to be careful because vodka put them (except Savénko and Galánin, whose sense of responsibility upheld them) in a quietly boisterous mood; and Martin, in spite of his lieutenancy, was the natural scapegoat and "object of fun." He was also their main channel for contact with the other residents in the hotel. When the day had gone well they toasted "peace," "friendship," and "international relations," with innumerable combinations and variations of these and with much merriment and suppressed titters. The toasts, which dragged on and on, were a way of filling in time and an excuse for swilling back the vodka *do dna* ("bottoms up"). For Martin there were trying moments, though they remained on good terms. This was, after all, his job. In time he earned their trust, even that of Stárov—when he was sober—by sometimes being deliberately awkward and gauche. Otherwise, when he was his natural Western self, Stárov tended to stare suspiciously at him.

As they sat, chatting and drinking, they were a special focus of attention. Couples turned to stare as they waltzed past. Most of the occupants of the hotel had never been to the Soviet Zone or to Vienna. But the members of the Mission seemed hardly to notice the long looks they received. It was as if inwardly they turned their backs on their surroundings; as if they had been—as they certainly *had* been, as Martin knew—warned against contamination by Western ways and ideas. Moreover, they always had to count with Galánin's watchful eye.

So it was that late one evening, when there were only a few couples left on the floor, Stárov—sitting squarely across the table, with his bull neck and beetling eyebrows—challenged Martin to see who could drink the most. Evidently, he had already been drinking heavily. His face was flushed, his tone boorish. But this time, while tentatively discussing the terms of the contest, Martin succeeded in steering the conversation away to the equally, or even more alluring topic of hunting (not D.P.s, but pheasant or duck), so that the challenge—which may well have been made by prior arrangement with the others, or at least with Galánin—was temporarily forgotten. It was Púnin, a hunting enthusiast, who vigorously seconded Martin's idea and helped change the subject.

They did not lose time. Less than a week after this, on a sparkling morning (it was early autumn), they arrived in Martin's Opel-Olympia and the jeep at the village of Ferlach at the foot of the Yugoslav Mountains. There they made their way to the sporting gun factory at the end of the village. They spent over an hour in a large upper room handling and testing rifles of every caliber and design, stroking the barrel, caressing their contours, and trying their feel and weight, amid the smell of well-oiled metal and much metallic clicking, before deciding which to buy. In the end they bought a twelve-bore rifle apiece and sufficient ammunition for several hunts. Spírin was glad to practice his German on the aproned assistant who showed them round. Stárov was like a child with a new toy. Martin watched him, recalling the occasion when he had first got the idea of the hunt, and wondered if hunting would in some way take the place of his earlier enthusiasm.

The night before the outing the two drivers were busy packing tins of caviar from the military stocks in Vienna, and bringing up fresh loaves from the Moser Hotel kitchen. All other activities were postponed for the day.

The next morning they set out before breakfast in the direction of Villach, drove along the bank of the Wërther See, past Velden, and headed for the mountains over a dirt path to a mountain lake. There, in a wild setting, they breakfasted in a hollow dip by the lake shore. They were all in high humor, especially Púnin, whom Martin referred to deliberately as the moving spirit behind the idea of the hunt.

They were driving, after breakfast, along the verge of the lake, admiring the scenery and the wild life, when the Colonel with his driver ahead in the jeep suddenly vanished from view round a turn. He had told the others to follow on behind for he was the only one with a large-scale map of the area. So they followed his trail until finally, exhausted by the speed they were forced to keep up, and losing the Colonel's track, they agreed to stop and await his return. They went down to the wide expanse of tall grass by the shore. The sun gleamed on the roof of a distant cottage high up on the mountainside, the only visible habitation. An occasional waterfowl ruffled the surface of the lake and disappeared among the reeds on the far shore. They moved stealthily behind Púnin over the marshy ground. But after about an hour of crouching and leopard-crawling, with some haphazard firing to try out their rifles, they decided—with no news of the Colonel—to return to Klagenfurt for lunch.

Half way through the meal, Savénko's driver turned up alone. He said the Colonel had gone off on foot, saying he would be back soon. He himself had dozed off at the wheel and when he woke up much later the Colonel was still nowhere to be seen, so he had come back to let the others know.

They set out again from the hotel after lunch, in the two cars, to try to retrieve the lost chief. But they had no success and by sundown they were back in Klagenfurt. It was after midnight when they were leaving the bar to retire for the night, still uncertain whether to inform the Austrian police about the disappearance of the Soviet Colonel (Martin even thought he might just possibly have been ambushed by vengeful D.P.s), that the lost chief suddenly turned up in the lobby, not looking the worse for wear, with his gun at the proper angle under his arm. He explained that he had walked on along the bank of the lake and had become so engrossed with the bird life that he had lost count of time. An Austrian car had given him a lift to the outskirts of Klagenfurt and he had walked the rest of the way. He looked flushed and happy; even, thought Martin, younger, in some way restored to life. From his belt hung three handsome spotted partridges. In spite of the setbacks and their tiredness, the other members of the Mission looked at him with amused pride, crowding round to examine the birds. That was their first abortive, or semi-abortive, attempt. They made a second, more serious, try at Grala, near Gratz, about half way to Vienna.

They spent the night at the small, gemüchklicht Transit Hotel at Gratz and the next morning rose before dawn, at half-past three.

The Colonel was already at his most perky, his short, lithe figure fussing round the hotel entrance in the dark, hustling everyone on, giving orders to sleepy hotel attendants as if they were Red Army units and he was organizing an assault. Stárov and Spírin came down late, bleary-eyed. Galánin had said he was not feeling well and would not come; Martin thought perhaps he was disillusioned with the first hunt.

They set out in two cars for Grala in the still raw morning. Dawn had not yet broken. They drove a long time through flat shrubby country and at last arrived at a log cabin and a row of wooden shacks. It was the hunting lodge of the Austrian Hauptmann they had visited some days before in his splendid country Schlöss to get permission for the use of his pheasant shoot. He had promised he would turn up himself, but he put in an appearance only at the end when they were already preparing to leave, just to check on the result.

In their enthusiasm they arrived early at the hunting lodge. The gamekeeper was still in bed and would not be woken. At that hour the place was dead except for the creeping rays of the first light of day that shone—as in an oriental painting—through the low-lying mist round the shacks. It was the chilliest hour of the morning. While they waited, muffled in their fur coats, they drank neat brandy in tumblerfuls and ate inch-thick caviar and cheese sandwiches. (It took a World War to produce sandwiches like that!) As they ate and drank they stamped up and down trying to keep warm, though the brandy and the rising sun soon produced their effect.

When the light cast a yellow veneer on the trees, the dry bracken, and the windows, there was movement inside. One window lit up like an awakened eye. Shortly after, the gamekeeper lumbered up to them round the corner of the log cabin. His face was lathered and he held a razor in his hand. "We'll get going at once," he said reassuringly. And before they even had time to climb into the cars, he was ready in full outfit, complete with Tyrolean hat and jaunty feather.

The sun shone promisingly as they started off. Savénko was in his element, grumbling at the lateness of the hour. On his face there was the look Martin had seen when he turned up late in Klagenfurt: the elation of the man of action, or of the reflective man of action; he was a complex character. On arrival at a large clearing they dismounted and counted the ammunition. Then they walked about a mile to the shoot. The gamekeeper showed them their places and warned them that on no account were they to fire at the chamoix (or *gam* in Austrian) as this was their mating season. Their prey was to be exclusively the male pheasant. So they moved around with, at first, something of the aimlessness which Martin remembered from Field Days in the Junior Training Corps at school. They fired sporadically and on meeting whispered a few words, holding smoking guns and re-loading.

Gradually, they adapted to the landscape and the hazy light. The whirring sounds of the pheasant rising from the bracken held everyone in a state of suspense. It was Martin's first real hunt and in this closeness to the physical world, their keen alertness and awareness, it seemed to him that they were reliving the experience of distant food-hunting ancestors. It was wonderful the way a hunt, at that early hour, at sunrise, could concentrate the senses and faculties. Never before had he felt so strongly this all-embracing absorption in nature. It was much more than just a mood; there was purpose and relatedness in their attentiveness, their movements. It made nature around them come more fully to life. It was a reality which had—in *this* way—previously escaped his notice. They were not just *in nature*; they were *with it, of it,* caught up in its obscure and tingling purposes. What remained of the morning haze contributed to this sense of enchantment. Martin focused so wholeheartedly on the immediate task that in a lapse of awareness he fired at, and almost shot, a chamoix. Luckily, it trotted off and vanished before he could reload and raise his gun. He looked around, but nobody had noticed.

After some hours, carrying the game, they returned to the clearing where they had left the cars and equipment. They placed the birds and hares in a wide semicircle, such as one sees in old photographs. Appropriately, Sávenko had got the most. The rest of them had nothing much to boast of. The tough Stárov, surprisingly, had nothing. He looked glum and shamed. Martin had only one hare, which barely saved his honor; but as he soon found out, that was to be his destiny with the Mission. They stood solemnly in line behind the birds while the gamekeeper took their photo. At first Sávenko made a show of objecting to being photographed. Martin knew he was worried about the Soviet regulation that no photographs must be taken of army personnel. But when Hauptmann, who had just arrived, insisted that he must have a copy for himself, he reluctantly gave way.

On their return to Graz they discussed the details of the hunt, commenting particularly on the Colonel's outstanding prowess. Sávenko himself was delighted with his performance: six pheasant, the bulk of their catch. Over dinner, they consumed four of the pheasant, and the air of satisfaction and celebration continued later at the bar of the Graz Hotel. In the early hours, when the local orchestra had packed up for the night, Major Stárov, who had been acting strangely after the day's outing, remembered the bet they had made—or he, Stárov, had made—in Klagenfurt as to who could drink the most, he or Martin. He was already tipsy, and somewhat piqued, Martin thought, by his poor performance as a huntsman, and perhaps by Martin's modestly face-saving showing. With blurred conviviality he mumbled: "What about our little bet?" His eyes were glassy and he tried to stare Martin down. Just then the abstinent Galánin, fresh from his day's rest at the hotel (Catching up with correspondence? Totting up the accounts?) turned up with two bottles of vodka under his arm which he placed on the table with an air of self-satisfaction.

Martin had only two or three times before tasted vodka, and never more than a glass. He knew nothing about its aftereffects when drunk unaccompanied by titbits of food or *zakuski*. There was a small plateful of salted fish on the table but this soon ran out; and the waiter said there was no more available. The bottle continued to make the rounds. The custom is that once a bottle is uncorked it must be finished. Stárov made sure that Martin's glass was filled to the brim each time. It was Martin who had originally suggested the hunt, so he could hardly draw back now at the time of celebration.

As always, they drank repeated toasts to "mutual friendship and understanding"—"*vechno*" (eternally), added Martin, already feeling his faculties weakening. He had never understood what pleasure people get from heavy drinking. He knew from experience what a poor drinker he was and how wretched were its aftereffects. Other than enhancing a fleeting moment of self-forgetful rowdiness or companionship, there seemed to be no redeeming feature in it. Moreover, drinking to excess did not put him in the high-spirited mood associated with drink, but the reverse; it made him sluggish and moody.

Stárov, though, continued to stare at him, and Galánin too, as if they were conniving at his downfall, nudging on the others with glances and stifled laughter.

Afterwards, Martin remembered only that late into the night, when the dance floor was a steady whirling vortex and he could no longer distinguish between the faces round him, following some obscure instinct of self-preservation, he rose unsteadily, proposed a final unintelligible toast, half-raising a full glass and then upsetting it over the table, muttering an apology and general good-night, and walked, or willed himself to walk—for he was not conscious of his legs—across the dance floor and past the bar to the exit. Summoning every ounce of his then almost non-existent self-control, he was just able to save the prestige of his uniform, his rank, and of the Empire on which still, for just a few more years, the sun would not set.

Next morning he rose very late, took a shower, and they met again at lunch. To his surprise, his relation with the members of the Mission had not only not deteriorated, they seemed to have improved. He was welcomed with smiles of complicity; like old soldiers, they had got drunk together. Martin's personal brand of the "stiff upper lip" had amused and even perhaps impressed them. There was nothing like a graceful "loss of face" to ingratiate oneself with men like Stárov, though Martin thought he detected a gleam of triumph in Stárov's eye, as if he, and Galánin, had made him pay for Stárov's humiliation in the hunt. But this, thought Martin, may just have been his imagination.

There was a Music Festival on at Gratz (part of the British Council's promotion of English culture), and the evening before their return to Klagenfurt they went to see Benjamin Britten's new opera *Peter Grimes* at the small local Opera House. It was in German and the music seemed strident and unfamiliar to the Mission. Nor was Martin so English (except in upbringing and education) that he could not share with them this particular distaste. For the Russians, though, it was probably just one more confirmation of Western decadence: an expression of "formalist" art. It was one more signal of a tottering Empire, beside which even their planned degradation of the previous evening—Martin's inability to take more than seven glasses of vodka—was a mere trifle. Anyway, as Savénko, the representative of the Mission, pointed out, and as Martin agreed, it was all as nothing compared to the pure joys of the hunt.

Joseph Patron, a resident of Spain, was born in Gibraltar in 1925. He has a PhD from Oxford (Trinity College), speaks French, Russian, Italian, Spanish and English, and is widely-traveled. Dr. Patron has taught on the college level in the USA and Italy and been associated with publishers in England, Italy and the USA. His articles, poems and stories are published mainly in England; his travel books have been published in Italian translation.

"Just don't get the idea that the present obligates you."

Night Shift

BY FAKIR BAYKURT

THE inside of the foundry was broader than the giant Munich Railroad Station. But it seemed confining to Ökkesh Tosun. He was fed up with plugging along and there were still a whole twenty minutes before he finished the night shift. In all that dust and smoke he couldn't see his hand in front of his face.

Yozgatli Hüseyin brought up the cart loaded with motor bearings. "File 'em, buddy! I brought you some more!" he said to Ökkesh Tosun.

Not only from under his arms, the sweat was also pouring from Ökkesh's waist and crotch. They expected fifteen pieces to be finished per hour. He was putting out seventeen or eighteen. These parts that he picked up, put on the tray, filed down, then lowered to the cart, weighed sixty kilos. If he pushed it, he could do twenty, but there was no enjoyment in that. He was thoroughly fed up with this damn night shift. It hadn't helped anyone's morale when an 18 x 52 white-hot lathe slipped from the winch chain and in a second smeared Konya Bekir's brains on the dusty ceiling. How many times had such things happened? And always on the night shift.

Sosyalist Ilhami, a machinist apprentice from Izmir, had repeated again and again: "There is an industrial accident in West Germany every six seconds! Of these, 69% are on the night shifts! Most of them involve foreign workers! And among those, most happen to Turks! Dwell on the meaning of this! Take some preventive measures! Today it happens to him, tomorrow to you! They call these accidents! And in Germany they don't let you know ahead of time that accidents are coming!"

For three or four days after the death they all sigh and lament, for three or four days they grumble. After they've kicked in forty or fifty marks to ship the body back home, they are as silent as a grave.

"Oh, how can you follow up and take precautions, Ilhami Efendi? Most of them hang a charm under their underwear! They have put their trust in God! Oh, how can you take precautions, brother?"

Once more Ökkesh Tosun decided to follow his own judgment. He would save himself by himself and that's all there was to it!

He was going to give one of the wall carpets, that he had brought back on his last leave, to Dilaver, his son's future father-in-law, and one to Meister Theo. Leaves had already started to become rarer. Gifts for this one, gifts for that. Whomever you gave a small present envied the one to whom you gave the bigger one. You couldn't please anybody. They look at you like creditors. You keep on getting deeper in debt! And you couldn't come back from Turkey empty-handed either. Slippers for this one, raki for that! Fancy village stockings, gold-embroidered jackets for the others...They wouldn't like it if you brought Turkish Delight candy...Enough now! There's absolutely no sense in prolonging this stupidity!

Ökkesh had put two marks in one of the luggage lockers at the giant railroad station and locked the carpet wrapped in plastic inside it. The key was now in his pocket. He wiped his hands on some waste and walked to Meister Theo's office at the front end. He had kept his eyes open for a week. Many had brought Turkish Delight and raki liquor, but no one at all had brought a carpet. Efendi Theo would be very pleased. He rehearsed to himself what he would say.

"I beg your pardon. This is a custom in our country. You think of those you like and respect. How many years we have worked here with you like brothers? I've never had even an angry look. You've smiled, Okkez Okkez! And treated me well. Don't get any ideas. It's nothing much. Around Anteppe we have one foot in Syria anyway. I brought one of those carpets you've seen on television. It's poor manners to say it but it's not imitation, it's good quality. If you hang it in your parlor it would go well. Believe me, Respected Meister, there's a lot of idle talk among us and some may say bribe. They would think that I expect something. Thank God I'm comfortable around here. Why should I ask for more? I brought it simply because I like and respect you. You know that I have a deep fondness and respect for you. I can't give it to you at the factory. I don't know your house. If I did I couldn't come there. Your wife might not understand. I put it in one of those luggage lockers at the station that you call *Schliessfach*. The letter and number is written on the key. Take it, throw it into the trunk of your car, and off to your house in Schwabing! Just don't get any ideas. This is not because I want to trick you, it's just because of my respect."

Meister Theo was sitting in the chair behind his desk. He had opened a one kilo bottle of apple juice which he was drinking straight from the bottle.

"Oh, Okkez! You're here?"

"Yes, here I am, Respected Meister."

His sweaty shirt was stuck to his back. He coughed. He started to speak, but he couldn't explain as he had rehearsed it in Turkish.

"No bribe, or anything! A little present. You'll see, Germany will make a decision and I'll have to pick up and leave. Let there be a reminder of me on the wall of your house. Say, 'Okkez Okkez!' and remember your friend. It's a little present so small that it fit into the luggage locker at the station. But you will be pleased with it. Here's the key. Just keep it between us. Some things are best kept secret. Just don't get the idea that the present obligates you. The only thing I expect from you is a smile and a kind word. I'm not saying take me off the night shift and put me on days. Your kindness is enough."

"Oh, Okkez! I've always known that you are a very good worker. What need is there for this? A wall carpet you say. But please, Okkez, wasn't it very expensive for you?"

"Haha, haha," he laughed politely. "How could your worth ever be compared with a carpet? Should a wall carpet be even the subject of conversation in your presence? I'm completely happy with you in this world and the next! Also, our factory in this city of Munich is in the *Allach Quarter*. May *Allah* be pleased with you! Our religions are different but we get better pay from you! Our own government couldn't do for us what you've done. Our own factories and companies, our own big shot bosses couldn't do it either! Anyway, take this key, my Esteemed Meister, I'm just about to drown in sweat! Talking here in your presence, I'm putting out all the sweat I didn't lose at work. Take the key!"

Theo quickly stood up and came over to Ökkesh. With his left hand he patted his shoulder, with his right he gripped his hand.

"You're a good employee, a good friend! I want very much to see your Turkey. My wife also. One vacation we'll go, perhaps..."

"Ah, dear Meister. If you'll only come! I'll have them beat the drums and blow the pipes in your honor. I'll have all of Anteppe and Kahramanmarash rise to their feet for you! I will never let you and your wife be disappointed, dear Meister!"

Meister Theo shook Ökkesh's hand again.

Ökkesh was soaked with sweat. He left hurriedly and said to himself, "Whether it works or not, it's my fate anyway in the end! We took care of this one, O.K.! When I've given the second one to that fanatic future father-in-law of my son, all will be well." There were fifteen minutes until the end of the shift. "I think I'll go and finish a couple more pieces!"

He raised the heavy casting, put it on the tray, and started to file.

Meister Theo cleaned up, dressed, and left together with the workers. His office, with the colored nude picture of Margaret, he turned over to his comrade, Johannes. He picked up his car from the parking lot and drove off.

Flowing along with the flood of traffic on the smooth local roads, he headed directly for the city center. It was hard to find a parking spot near the station. As a matter of fact it was hard to find a parking place in the whole city, all the cities. When he immediately saw an empty spot behind the taxis at the front entrance he jumped for joy. "I'm lucky in some things! Even if my marriage is a little faded!"

Feeling sorrow for the good years that were spent and gone with plump Karen, he unlocked the luggage locker on the left and took out the plastic-wrapped carpet. "Oh!" he sighed, "this is going to have a happy effect on Karen."

He carried the carpet to the car and put it into the trunk. Then he took the road to his home in Schwabing. In the morning gloom the place was filled brimful with people going to or returning from work, students, and also American soldiers. He parked his car in the usual place on the street. With the carpet under his arm he climbed the stairs. The apartment where they lived was new. He found it best not to ring the bell to his flat on the third floor. Perhaps Karen was still sleeping. The house key was on the same ring as his car keys. As usual he found it and stuck it in the keyhole.

They had one child, Konrad, who had got up, had breakfast, and was about to leave with his bag for school. Konrad was in the second grade. Theo kissed his son. "Good-bye, my boy," he said and closed the door. He took off his clothes and leaned the carpet against the parlor wall. He would take down the picture of the snow-covered Swiss Alps and hang it in its place. "When Karen awakes we'll hang it together," he said. He went to the basin in the bathroom, turned on the hot water, soaped a washcloth and squeezed it. He rubbed it on his arms, under his armpits, and on his neck and stomach. Then he walked into the bedroom in his birthday suit. Karen was lying on her stomach. He crawled into his side of the bed and thought, If I pet her she'll get angry now! She makes me go astray! If she'd only wake up and give me a hot embrace! If I touch her she'll wrinkle up her nose...

Karen awakened. "Is that you, Theo?"

"Probably."

"Are you home?"

"Probably am."

She forced a smile. "Are you well, Theo?"

"I'm very well. How are you?"

"I had a bad dream, Theo."

The sweet hill where her hip joined her waist caught his eye. It was very pleasant to look at. He gently caressed it with his hand. Karen quickly turned over.

"What time is it?"

"Past seven."

"Did you put on the coffee?"

"I'll go put it on if you like."

"Don't go! Lie down a while! What's new?"

"A present."

"Not raki again."

"No, not raki again."

"I'm fed up with the Turks' raki and their Turkish Delight. I don't drink it, you don't drink it! Konrad doesn't eat the candy either. I keep on taking the bottles and boxes to neighbors and friends. It's plain on their faces that they don't like what they get either."

From time to time Theo gave some to a Turkish engineer who worked at Siemens. He had chanced across Erhan in a beer garden nearby. In order to be able to get rid of two bottles of Klup or Altinbash raki, he had to invite him home for coffee. But now let her see the carpet and watch how surprised she'll be!

"A little gift..." He hadn't told her it was a carpet yet so her surprise would be complete. He expertly changed the subject. But Karen didn't linger long in bed. It would be better if she fixed coffee and breakfast herself.

Theo decided to get up later after sleeping a little while. He closed his eyes.

Karen looked on the table. There was no raki bottle, nor a box of Turkish candy, nor a package of slippers either. She quickly walked to the sitting room. There it was by the wall wrapped in plastic. She went back, got the kitchen scissors and snipped the cord. "Oh my God!" she said. "Someone finally thought of it! It's a small carpet. But I wonder what the design is?" She loved one with a deer she had seen at a friend's. "After this it will rain such carpets; we've got it made! Choose whichever one you want! Theo is a well-liked Meister." She unwrapped the carpet. She would look at it and then let out a squeal of delight.

But suddenly the opposite happened. She wrinkled up her face in a frown. She gathered somehow that this was the Sultan Ahmet Mosque and Obelisk in Istanbul—but she was a bit foggy. However, in that foggy perception her mind flashed: Could there be a little dirty trick involved in this introduction of a carpet with minarets into a Christian home? "I don't think so," she said to herself. "They couldn't manage that." She laughed softly: "Poor Theo! Who knows how much he suffers working with these insensitive laborers? Let's say we hang this on the wall. Our friends and acquaintances, neighbors and relatives, including my father's family, will say, 'What's going on? Has our Theo worked so long with the Turks that he's becoming a Moslem? And you Karen, do you close your eyes to this?' Not in this world can I hang such a carpet on the wall in my home!" She put the carpet down. As if it were made of silk, the 110 x 180 carpet draped softly over the divan.

Karen put butter and cheese on the table. She set out the coffee glasses. The coffee was slowly filtering. She went to the bathroom and washed her mouth. She washed herself with a cloth.

At eight-thirty she had to rush off to work. She entered the bedroom naked. "Hey, Theo! Breakfast's ready. Get up!" she said. "Hurry, get up!"

Theo only half heard her. Karen walked out to the parlor. Suddenly her face lit up. She went to the toolbox and found a hammer and nails. "I'll hang it and let him see just what kind of a carpet it is!" She took down the Swiss snow scene, folded the carpet in two and hung it on the wall. "I'll hang it that way so he'll think it's an abstract," she said.

Theo got up; scratching himself, he walked into the kitchen.

Karen went to the bedroom and got partly dressed. She came and poured their coffee. "I'm late again, Theo!" She was ill-tempered, as always.

"You saw the present, didn't you?"

"I saw it."

"Well, didn't you like it?"

"It's nice. I hung it on the wall."

"Is that so?"

"No, I'm joking..."

"Well, it's a nice wall carpet, isn't it?"

"Probably."

"Okkez, the man who brought it is very nice. He works as a filer. He says, 'Come to our country and we'll entertain you, how we'll entertain you!' Let's go there on our vacation—if you want to."

Karen was going to say, "Isn't there any other place left in the world?" But she didn't want to spoil her husband's good mood and contained herself. "I have to catch the streetcar, Theo! Kafka Street's a long way! I have to be there right at nine. I can't keep the bank customers waiting."

Theo walked slowly to the sitting room. He looked at the wall. The gift had been hung in place of the snow-covered Swiss mountains. It's colors were very attractive. But it was a little confused. Had the reflection of the trees fallen into a lake. He didn't study it long. The sparkle of the attractive colors were enough for the first look. He returned to the kitchen: "He not only brings a carpet but doesn't want anything in return! I like him very much." He took a sip of coffee. Then he winked at his wife. "He works on the night shift."

"Their religion decrees that, I think," Karen said. "But wait, you're going on the day shift soon. Take him on the new shift with you. Who knows how happy he will be."

"Listen, Karen! If you want we can go in the summer! They say it's very cheap in Turkey. That is with our money. If you want we can fly; it's too hard by car."

"Anyway, excuse me, Theo, I must go."

"The reflection of the trees in the water is beautiful, isn't it?"

"Bravo!" Karen said. "I didn't figure that out."

When Ökkesh Tosun discovered that the carpet he had left at home was the one with the deer, he was worried to death. His son, Bülent, had reached his twenties. They had chosen Emine, the daughter of Dilaver from Kaghizman, to be his bride. They had decided to go to Cologne on the Sacrifice Holiday to ask for her hand. His future father-in-law was truly very devout. The carpet with the mosque was just the thing to court his approval. How had he given it to the Meister? How had he been so absent-minded?

From morning till night he lay in bed groaning and lamenting. He couldn't sleep at all. His upper and lower eyelids never touched. The neighborhood kids were raising a rumpus to the skies. But this last catastrophe was worse than all of them.

"You dumb jackass, Ökkesh, how could you make this mistake?"

He thought of blaming the whole thing on his wife, Gülizar, and giving her a good scolding. But when he went to work the day before, he had taken it with his own hand. He had taken the carpet and locked it in one of the lockers in the giant railroad station. How could he rebuke her?

He tossed and turned in bed. He couldn't get one wink of sleep. He didn't know what to say or what to do. "As far as the German is concerned it makes no difference. A carpet is a carpet. But how can I give the one left with a deer to that fanatic who's going to be my son's father-in-law? The one with the mosque would have gone over well. Dumb Ökkesh, look at this silly thing you've done!"

In the afternoon when he woke up and pulled himself together, he still had the problem of the carpet with the mosque on his mind. He burned and writhed in bed. Then suddenly he shivered as if a holy inspiration had been born in his heart.

"At the very most it will only cost me two more marks! Tonight I'll take the one with the deer and put it in the luggage locker. Again I'll give the key to the Meister! I'll beg his pardon and say, 'There were two. One for him and one for the father-in-law to be, Dilaver! I'll tell him candidly. He's not going to kill me! That's the way a man is, he can make more than one mistake. This new way of life scrambles your brains. Let him put the mosque carpet in and give me the key. I will have gone one more time to the station where my foot first touched German soil."

He went back to sleep. In his dream he saw that his shift had changed from night to day and he was happy. That being taken care of, he also believed that the business of getting his son married was going well.

Born in 1929, in Akcha, Fakir Baykurt has become one of Turkey's great short story writers and novelists. He specializes in social comment about Turkey's villages and peasants. His translator, Joseph S. Jacobson, is a university professor who has translated several Turkish stories for scholarly journals.

"I stood over him, fists balled, grinding my teeth one instant, screaming at him the next."

Who's to Say This Isn't Love?

BY WILLIAM PITT ROOT

IT was exactly twenty-seven miles to the doctor, and there wasn't a mile without a pair of switchbacks or a hairpin combination tight enough to make a well man gasp and pale. Red Dog was not what you'd call a well man. I had no intention of sparing him the least of those curves. I had the perfect excuse, at last. I was saving his life.

Red Dog, which is how he liked to be called, from his navy days, was both just then—red as a beet with strangulation, sick as a dog from his latest drunk. He was having an asthma attack, and he'd run out of whatever it was he usually took to bring him around. My mother, his wife, had called ahead to the doctor. I was to deliver Red Dog to the clinic, as quickly as possible. Which was just fine by me.

I was twenty, home from school for the summer. For wheels, I had a '53 Ford convertible, electric blue, with white tuck-and-roll naugahyde upholstery that would pass for leather, until you ran your hand over it. I loved it, loved sitting in it and daydreaming, loved taking off into the California coastal hills on a sunny day with the top down and radio blaring, tearing into these curves like I was crazy to die. And I was, in those days.

So when my mother called me by sending my twelve-year-old sister down to the beach, you can be sure I was ready. "He can't breathe," she gasped, breathless herself after the three-block run from the house. By the time I got there Mother had him sitting on the steps outside the radio shack where he spent most of his time. The shack was exactly that, set apart from the house itself, a kind of island in the backyard. It was loaded with radio gear that got Red Dog in touch with other hams all over the world while his wife sat in the kitchen chainsmoking and probably dreaming how one day he'd come out that door and talk to her like he talked to "The Limey" in Sussex or the guy in Teaneck, New Jersey, the one with the prostate problem, or any of the other air voices with whom he could cheerfully exchange all the thoughts and feelings he would boil down to "Hey, get me another beer, will you, hon?" when he spoke to his wife, my mother.

He looked awful. His face was splotchy red and white and his lips were blue. A patriot. The veins across his temple were distended and his eyes were bright and frantic. He gave me his drowning look, the look he reserved for when he was smashed and telling his war stories or when he'd got himself in a jam I was supposed to get him out of.

We got him to the car and I slammed the door and locked it to be sure he wouldn't go tumbling out on the first hard curve. The top was already down. My mother was hovering over him, clearly regretful at missing this chance to be needed by him, to help him in a way she knew. But one of the babies was sick and even for this she couldn't leave. And I was the fast driver. Actually, of course, it wasn't as serious as it seemed. I mean who ever dies of asthma? To my way of thinking at the time, it was just a grownup's version of the child-holding-its-breath, a tantrum the subconscious threw when a couple of neural lines, probably overloaded originally decades ago, accidentally crossed and short-circuited. Like I said, I was twenty, I'd been off to school. I'd read some things.

 "Not too fast," she tried to call out after the car as I took off, deaf and determined. I was on a mission. Old Red Dog had talked missions plenty of times to me, making sure I understood I'd never had anything more important than a dentist's quarter hour depending on me in my life. Now it was different. By the time I hit the town-limit sign at the edge of the bay, half a mile from the front gate of the house, he knew. At first he tried feebly to wave a hand to signal me to slow down, but I could sense in him the moment he grasped it, the situation I mean, and he let his hand flutter back into his lap like a semaphore flag whose handle had snapped. As soon as he recognized his helplessness, he decided to cut his losses. I had to respect that.

In fact, there *was* one mile that was almost straight where the two-lane blacktop followed the bay shore to the intersection with Highway 1. We hit that intersection going just under ninety. The legal limit was thirty-five. There was an old yellow pickup half a mile south, nothing else, and we went through that intersection like a hound with a half-pint of red-eye up his ass. Which was one of Red Dog's sayings. He had a million.

A lot of those expressions, which I would later recognize for the service clichés they were, struck me at the time, for all their vulgarity, as clearly richer and more effective than the catch phrases of my peers. Most of those trumped-up inanities already have vanished from my memory, leaving only an aftertaste so vapid I have to admit Red Dog was right about us. We were snot-nosed kids. We were the ones lucky enough to avoid the draft before most of us really grasped that Vietnam could become anything but an inconvenient delay in our oblique quest for a secure spot just left of center in the middle class we thumbed our noses at. King was already on the march to the mountaintop. Rockwell, the Nazi, openly inveighed against "niggers and jews;" Rockwell, the industrial manufacturer, still could safely keep the minority employees "in their place." The Beatles were just catching on, the Stones were still unthinkable, Alice Cooper was not old enough to catch the second generation "You Bet Your Life" reruns.

But sometimes Red Dog got things curiously backwards. Or so it seemed to me at the time. The summer before, when I'd come back from school (in response to my mother's plea that I come stay with her to protect her from Red Dog while she got a divorce), he'd known what was in the air. He looked at me like looks should kill so he wouldn't have to waste a bullet. We got right into it.

"How you like college?" he said, but now without looking my way.

"It's O.K. with me." Never one to be caught without a snappy reply, from the shoulders of Nietzsche, Fichte, Spinoza, Wilde.

"Well, I'll tell you what, you snot-nosed piece of shit," he began, a metaphor that would have left Kilmer, for all his ingenuity at mangling, slack-jawed. "I'll just tell you what. When the gooks take over this place, and believe me, they will, and when they do they're going to take all you snot-nosed college kids and chain your asses to machine guns—then you'll see just how it is." He glared. "You'll think of me then, and you'll say, 'The Chief was right. He knew what he was talking about. He told me how it was.'"

Now I'd only laid eyes on Red Dog a few times before. He'd done his courting by having my mother meet him down at the CPO Club, surreptitiously, you might say. I'd met him, of course, briefly, I on my best behavior, he on his, each equally deceptive, friendly. Two years later my mother married him to get him out of the alcoholic ward of the VA Hospital in southern California, where he was facing court-martial. Before that, when she got pregnant, he'd skipped the country and only answered her letters when he ended up stateside in the lockup, urging her to give him the chance to give his daughter a name. Which she did, against her own better judgment as well as mine. A name's a name. What I'm saying is he had taken me aback.

"So just how is it?" I countered, foolishly.

And that is how we got into the duel with bayonets that first night I was home. I'd had a bayonet ever since my real father gave me one when I was a little kid. And I could throw it, let me tell you. So when he challenged, choice of weapons was mine. I chose bayonets and for the first time he smiled a real smile. I knew I was in trouble. He knew I knew. There was no backing down. Not my first night home.

"Jim," my mother, his wife cried. He did have a Christian name. "Don't be—" and for a second I had the notion she was going to accuse him of being rude, "like that," she finished, tears welling. I didn't know it at the time, but she was pregnant again.

At sunset, as agreed, I waited for him in the backyard, and he saved my life. I had it all planned. When he approached he'd have to pass a certain tree. I'd already tested the range, sinking the bayonet two inches into the meat of the trunk after a double flip. When he came I'd nail him right there. But he didn't come. Either way he saved my life—by not killing me, by not letting me kill him. He saved me by getting sloshed and passing out in bed. That I found out later. It didn't matter. I admit it. I was glad.

But it did seem to me he'd gotten things mixed up, using the "gooks" as his henchmen in the threat. He wasn't going to show me, he was going to let *them* show me. Like they were his guys. And it wasn't until the duel that we got back on the right track, if you can call it that.

"So how you doing? Can you breathe?"

He was laying his head back against the seat, staring up at the sky twisting and turning overhead as I negotiated the preliminary curves heading into the hill range. I didn't want him going to sleep. I didn't want him to miss a thing.

He began working his mouth but no sound came out. No sound loud enough to be heard over the roar of wind sucking down behind the windshield anyhow. Fish out of water is what he looked like. One of those big goldfish with yellow mouths sipping at the top of the pond. Red Dog had red hair, pink skin, red lips, blue eyes. When he drank the blue would wash out. He'd look at me with those milky eyes and tell me some story. The stories were interesting, I had to give him that. Interesting the first three or four times.

One he liked to tell was about being torpedoed in the South Pacific in World War II and spending three days and two nights in the water, him and fifteen hundred other men. Fifteen hundred other men to start. By the end something like two hundred eighty. I guess there weren't enough boats for everyone, or the ship just sank too fast. So they were hanging on to anything, the flotsam and jetsam, although he never would've called it that, and at night he said you could hear the guys keeping track of each other, calling out and all, and then he said you'd hear a scream. And you'd know it was the sharks. All night. And it was beautiful, he said. Stars, the moon, and there wasn't anything you could do.

First they'd call out questions, encouragements, then it was just names. "Johnson, here." "Horowitz, yo." "Shannihan here." Then a scream. "Johnson, here." "Horowitz, here..." and you'd know. You'd know, but there wasn't anything you could do. By the second afternoon some of the men were too exhausted to fight off the gulls and the gulls would just land on a guy and peck out his eyes and often as not the guy would just be staring straight ahead by then, like he was looking at something, and the gulls would just do it. Then the night again. He said by the end there wasn't anybody who wasn't crying. Looking up at the stars. By the end two hundred eighty, I think that was the number, were rescued and he was one. He told me this one a lot, at the CPO Club.

The first time he told it, when he finished he looked pretty bad, and I put my hand on his hand on the bar. He looked at me, and he really put it to me.

"Do you like me?" he asked.

"Sure. Sure, I like you." What else could I say? Besides, just at that moment I did like him. Something like that. I knew him, which is as good. Or so I thought.

"Do me a favor?" he says.

And I say, "Name it."

"Call me 'Dad'."

I felt sick. I think he could have asked me almost anything else just then, and maybe I would've done it, just then, like it was. But that. That was the one thing. And I looked at him and he knew it, and I hated his guts for asking me that when he knew what it was. He knew exactly—right through his drunk, right through his story, he knew.

"I can't. You know I can't." And the son of a bitch watched me with the tears in my eyes I couldn't brush away without him seeing.

Right at the start, at the first good curve, he had thrown his right hand up along the top of the door to steady himself; when finally, miles later, his left hand rose in an involuntary gesture to get me to slow down, I didn't see a thing. The trees crowding the road along this stretch blurred into a mess of running greens and the poppies by the roadside streaked by like golden dashes if you looked at them. I loved those poppies, the way they could retain the light at twilight, glowing equally, perfectly, from each petal. At this speed trying to see them was like trying to decipher the graffitti on a subway roaring by.

Which is how a lot of things seem to me now. At twenty, everything seemed eternal in its passage, every object a symbol eager to yield up meaning, every face a face you would know always—whether to hate it or to love it hardly mattered next to that unexamined assumption of its permanence in your life. But the faces, the amused or hateful or loving faces, that once held light like wine in crystal, have a way of running into each other, calling out to one another in the dark or in dreams, screaming or suddenly vanishing without a sound; and they turn into stories, in order not to disappear altogether, and the stories are entirely at the mercy of memory in which the tides of need may shift, unpredictably, at any hour. A certain plea, heard at twenty, is obscene; a few years later, it seems, almost, to have been a prayer.

And so we tore through a gathering twilight which has continued to darken through all these years since, slowly, slowly, him hanging onto that locked door and full of the ghosts who could creep out of him only when drunkenness permitted rage or tears to blast open the gates or when the vast electrical spaces conducting anonymous air voices let him blunt the edge of his isolation against that of others—all this in threats, trivia, whining, the calculated plea—until his throat would seize around it rather than release it into such a world, such a people.

But at that time, careening through those woods, over the crests of those hills which left our bellies hung like kites in the air as we plunged downward and on, and his grip on the door tightened, his hand white as his face—at that time, I thought it was all up to me. I thought I could give him his own back again. I thought I had the wheel.

I was a good driver. Stupid, but still good at staying on the road. Too good, as it turned out. Halfway there, he turned to me, his face by that time green as the trees behind him.

"You're one hell of a driver."

I looked over at him.

"What'd you say?"

"Hell of a driver," he wheezed, his smile ghastly as a death's head. "Keep it up."

Keep it up. I stepped on the gas, grim. But the fact is, it pleased me to hear him say that. It wasn't what I wanted, to be pleased. I wanted him to beg me to slow down, I wanted him to lean over that door he clung to and throw up his whole damned life. Ridiculous. After all those years aboard ships, a little motion sickness wasn't going to be in the cards. Years later, on my first trip at sea, I threw up and I thought of him, that way he had of walking like he still was on deck, bow-legged, ready to go to this side or that for balance, if the earth shifted. And the first time I had to work for a real SOB, I remembered Red Dog's story of him and another Chief throwing a snot-nosed Lt. JG overboard in a storm. After months of his riding them and all the other old hands too hard, they drew straws. Matches, I mean. "Man overboard," Red Dog called, an hour after the splash.

I pushed the Ford too hard finally and spun out and we both ended up just about in each other's arms by the time we came out of it and I got the car tracking again. At first I assumed he was wheezing, and he was, but the wheeze was his laughter, the closest he could get to it then. I almost started to laugh, too. But even when he laughed his eyes were wrong. I mean he had that way of watching you even when he was dead drunk, even when he was laughing.

When I came home from swing shift that time and found him alone, glaring from his chair, and I asked what was going on, he wouldn't say a thing. He just glared, watching through the glare as through a one-way mirror. "Where's Mother?" Nothing.

Then she burst in, breathless, looking back and forth between us. "Did he tell you? What he did?" He had chased her out of the house with his Luger because she defended my sister—eleven at the time, my adopted sister—against his demand that she get out of the house within twenty-four hours, because, he said, her mother had been a whore for a French troopship and he didn't want her in the same house with him. The story came out fast but by the time my mother, his wife, had it told, I was on my feet, explosive, and I lifted the coffee table in front of me and threw it across the room at him where he sat, drunk, watching me. It was a flimsy thing and it glanced off the wall beside his chair and clattered to the floor, broken-legged. He just sat there watching, hating.

I stood over him, fists balled, grinding my teeth one instant, screaming at him the next.

"Do you know what you did, you son of a bitch, answer me, do you know what you've done to that kid?" I grabbed him and shook him, and he shook like a sack of laundry. No trace of resistance, nothing. I grabbed him by his red hair and pulled back his head and raised my fist, and he glared, watching. I couldn't do it. I couldn't punch him if he wasn't there for it, if he seemed almost to want it. I wouldn't work for him like that. So I stood there panting and heaving, and I told him to get out, sent him to the bedroom like a bad child, and he went.

By the time he came back I was numb, my rage was spent. He had the razor-knife from the warehouse he was working in those first days as a civilian, having beaten his court-martial for drunkenness by two weeks—a twenty-year-man, with nowhere left to go but out. He caught me in a corner of the room, with that knife weaving in front of me and a crazed brightness in his colorless eyes, and he said, "So, punk, you want to fight? You want to fight, let's fight. Let's see what you can do."

The first thing I did was order her out of there. "Get the cops," I added. She stared like she was mesmerized for a minute, then went out the front door.

"All right, punk," he began, "now, it's just you and me, just you and me, son." And he continued, working his way through his litany of hate-names for me and my kind, all the Lt. JG's in the world, the snot-nosed kids who'd pulled rank on him all his life. And with each new name he slashed nearer with the razor. Then it caught on my shirt, opened it like a paper wrapper.

I was ready. That's always surprised me, how quickly I was ready for that moment, as if I'd been waiting all my life for it. He had three inches on me in height and reach, and he had the knife, the literal edge. But I watched the knife, and I saw that the razor in it was extended only enough to slit open the cardboard cartons it was meant for, or my guts, if I let him reach them. He hadn't thought to extend the blade before he began waving it at me. Half an inch, maybe less. That meant he could slice me to ribbons, but no way could he kill me fast. And I knew before I would die, I could kill him, and would. I knew it, I saw it in my mind as in slow motion: he would reach forward to slash and as he slashed I would break his larynx with my fist. A sucker's swap. My blood, his life. When I spoke my voice was so transformed I knew he would hear the death in it.

"Touch me you're a dead man." And it was as if I had already done it, broken him. He looked at my eyes, not watching now, but looking. He looked at me, looked at the knife in his hand. He turned around and went back into the bedroom, without a word. After that, things changed. He was broken somewhere. He drank, drove the car off a bridge one night in the fog, ended up in jail. They let him off. It was all going fast now. Again, he got drunk, while I was at work in the factory, chased my mother and sister from the house with the Luger he couldn't even hold in his shaking hand. Jail again. This time she had him committed. The second child was born. Eighteen hours of labor, at her age, alone with only me there, alone without him. I went back to school, she left him, moved to the coast, tried to cover her tracks.

He found her once he was out, and she let him in like you'd let in a dog from a storm. But he was the storm as well as the dog. The older baby called him Daddy. By the time I saw him again, a year later, they both could say that: *Daddy, Daddy.* And he would hold them over his head and say, "What's happening?" Spin them. "What's happening?" Then he would disappear for days, drunk.

What did I know? It made no sense to me then, none of it. I married, too, and by the time we broke up nothing of that made sense to me either. I could tell something in me was destroying her, and she wanted me to stay and finish it. One bad night we were parked by the ocean, looking out over the waves coming in through the dark. She was crying. I held her. She knew it was over. She knew before I told her, but she wanted me to tell her and I did. She was crying and she liked to have me hold her. What could you do? Then she looked at me and even in the moonlight I could see her eyes dilate, cat-like, and a kind of cheer came into her face. I couldn't look away from those eyes whose tears I tasted in my mouth.

"I know what we can do," she said.

I looked at her, waiting.

"We can kill ourselves." I looked away from her after a minute, looked down into the waves with their silver linings answering only to the moon. "We can," she repeated. And that was what had been in her eyes. I felt my heart shrink. That's no figure of speech. When astronauts come back in from the void, their hearts are shrunken. No one knows why. It happens.

But by that time in my life, it had all begun to rush for me, everything, rushing by so fast that if you reach out to grab, something comes off in your hands—an arm, the collapsed mask of a face, memories forming almost before the events they recount have even occurred. And what can you do? It all goes by like wreckage in a river or faces in a plunging train, and if you grab there's carnage and if you don't there's nothing. So you end up in an eddy somewhere, maybe with someone. Maybe not. And it's your life. It's your life. He and my mother and the girls: his bottles, her cigarettes; his violence and asthma, her enlarged heart and bronchitis; his radio intricately glowing in the darkness of his shack, her eyes full of the night she looks down into from her window above the backyard where he carries on conversations with Lima and Toronto, her cigarette a dull red star in the window he turns his back on. Who's to say this isn't love?

So I had the wheel that time, when I still believed in the wheel and revenge, and rage was as pure as a songbird bringing up the sun. But as I raced he smiled, and the deathly silence of his smile was an avalanche that outsped my skill at anything I imagined I could do to him. I was not ready to die. He was. And death was close for him, but it was not in one of the tree trunks blurring by nor in any of the dusky drop-offs at the edge of the road. And it was not at the hand of a friend.

He told me that one only once. Korea, his best buddy on his knees in front of him as the dust cleared, leaving him stone-deaf for days afterwards. Red Dog knelt before the man, whose hands glistened in his own guts, more than even both of his hands could hold; and as he begged Red Dog—soundlessly, like a clip from a film in which something had gone wrong, some mechanical failure—he kept trying automatically to stuff them back into his drenched shirt as they lolled out over his hands like the heavy coils of a snake that would not be still. Red Dog shot him, between the eyes, as he looked at him, or through him, with the same gun his hand could not hold again against my mother, later. He didn't say it then, when he was telling the story; but later, drunk, when he would interrupt a silence with that question over and over, I would know.

"What is a friend for?" He made it sound like a riddle. "What. Is. A. Friend. For." And he would look into his hands open on the bar before him, squeeze them slowly closed, clenching his jaw as he did it, closing his eyes.

On the way back, after the doctor gave him the injection and he was himself again, there stood in the headlights a row of eucalyptus trees, their bark hanging from them in red loops. We were both getting drunk. I was driving slowly. The ranks of eucalyptus seemed to go on and on in the headlights as we drove beside them. I remarked that they looked like beggars in rags.

He looked at them a long while, and when he turned to me I imagined his eyes were brimming tears. "That's right, that's exactly what they look like," he said, and then he said, "Thank you, thank you for telling me that." I don't think I said anything. I was surprised. It was nothing.

In two years you were dead. In a rented room in an L.A. dive. Congestive heart failure, strangulation. My mother, your wife, had had you committed again, had escaped you again, this time to the City of Angels, as she called it when she first wrote to tell me her plan. You'd found her again, but this time she turned you away. This time she was ready to live. She turned you away without letting the girls see you and beg her for their daddy again. They never knew you had been there, a wool cap hiding the flap of scalp sutured over the plastic plate where your skull had been caved in during some brawl or in some alley where you had wakened to find a stranger's hand in your pocket. You couldn't remember. You'd been in a coma for weeks. You'd learned to speak again, to feed yourself, to walk short distances, your indomitable sea legs still there to hold you up when the earth shifted, as it did so often then.

"No more drinking, hon." How familiar for her the heartbreak of that promise must have been. "The docs said one drink," that's all she wrote. Standing in the porch-light at the foot of the stairs which she had come halfway down, so you wouldn't have to speak so loudly as to wake the girls, you shyly took off the cap to show her the gleaming, the way a kid might show off a frog, knowing others might find it repulsive, but knowing, nonetheless, what a prize it truly was. When they found you among the empty bottles in your room, they couldn't even determine how long you'd been dead. You were thirty-seven.

Now I am thirty-seven. King is dead, long live the King. The Nazi is dead, and the painter. JFK and Bobby. John Lennon is dead. And Penny Lane. The Stones are middle-aged millionaires. Alice Cooper was one of the last, perhaps the last, to comfort Groucho as he died. The list goes on. The list is hungrier than we are. One of your daughters is a nurse, always looking for the man she can heal. The other is the image of you, asks about you sometimes. We lie, and she loves you. We lie, and she knows, and she loves you. The young girl you ordered out of your house is a woman with her own home now, her own children, a strong woman who refuses marriage. Mother did not remarry, keeps her cats and dogs, keeps your name, keeps having difficulty breathing. One night in San Francisco, years ago, police took away my bayonet. Maybe it was time for that, because I was relieved to let it go. Later I read that along with all the other weapons confiscated that year it was melted down to be cast as a statue by Benny Bufano, the waterfront sculptor. And that's not all, you'll like this part—it's a statue of Christ welcoming sailors home from the sea.

William Pitt Root is a short story writer and well-published poet. Some of his work has been translated into Russian and broadcast by Radio Free Europe. His poems have appeared in England, Japan, Canada, as well as in numerous USA publications. This story is from his collection of stories Who's To Say This Isn't Love?.

"It was an elemental desire to establish a society of two."

Dancing on the Radio

BY PAUL THEROUX

FLORA Domingo-Duncan said, "I used to be a mess," and laughed, and said, "It was my mother. So I went to graduate school in California and put three thousand miles between us. God, am I boring!"

"You're not boring," I said.

"I don't want you to get sick of me."

"I'll never get sick of you."

We were naked in bed on our backs and speaking to the ceiling.

"Anyway, I was a wreck," she said, and clawed her blond hair away from her forehead. "I had a shrink. I wasn't embarrassed, I just didn't want to talk about it, so I told people I was seeing my dentist. Twice a week! 'You must have terrible teeth,' they'd say. But it was my mind that was a mess. Hey, why are we talking about my mind?"

Because during our lovemaking we had become very private and fallen silent. I thought then that no one was more solitary than during orgasm. We were resuming an interrupted conversation.

"I like your mind," I said. "I like your green eyes. I like your sweet et cetera."

"Good old E.E. Cummings." She was expert at spotting quotations. We agreed on most things, on *Wuthering Heights, To the Lighthouse, Dubliners,* and *Pale Fire;* on Joyce Cary, Henry James, Chekhov, and Emily Dickinson. We shared a loathing for Ernest Hemingway. That night we had gone to the National Theatre to see *La Ronde*, by Arthur Schnitzler; and then I made omelettes; and we went to bed, and talked about *La Ronde*, and made love. But literature was as crucial as sex—we were getting serious. Liking the same books made us equals and gave us hope; we had known the same pleasure and experience. Taste mattered: Who wanted to live with a philistine or to listen to half-baked opinions? Everything mattered. And there was her Mexican side, a whole other world. It was not exactly revealed to me, but I was aware of its existence. In all ways, with Flora, I seemed to be kneeling at her keyhole. She loved that expression.

It was spring, and the windows were open. The night-sweet fragrance of flowering trees was in the air.

"This is luxury," she said. She pronounced it *lugzhery,* because she knew I found it funny, like her comic pronunciation of groceries, *grosheries.*

"But I have to go," she said.

"Stay a while longer."

"Just a little while."

She lived off Goldhawk Road, at Stamford Brook, in two rooms. It was there that she worked on Mary Shelley, with occasional visits to the British Library. Her time was limited. She had only until July to finish her research; then back to the States and summer school teaching. She worked every morning, and so it was important to her that she left me at night.

"I have to wake up in my own bed," she said. "Otherwise I won't get anything done."

I admired her enterprise and her independence, but I was also a bit threatened by them—or perhaps made uneasy, because her life seemed complete. She had a Ph.D., an Oxford D.Phil., and was an assistant professor at Bryn Mawr. She was presently on a traveling fellowship, working on a biography of Mary Shelley. She was beautiful, and I never wanted her to go. She had never spent a whole night in my bed.

I said, "I wish you needed me more."

"That's silly. You should be glad I'm independent," she said. "I can see you more clearly. Don't you know how much I like you?"

I liked her. I craved her company. I liked myself better when I was with her. The word "like" was useless.

"But I need you."

"There's no reason why you have to say it like that," she said, smiling gently and kissing me. "Anyway, you have everything."

"I used to think that," I said.

She said, "It's scary, meeting someone you like. Friendship is scarier than sex. I keep thinking, 'What if he goes away? What if he stops liking me? What if...what if...?'"

"I'm not going anywhere."

"But I am," she said. She could be decisive. She kissed me and got out of bed and dressed quickly. And minutes later I was watching her car pull away from Overstrand Mansions and already missing her.

I had thought that once we were sexually exhausted we would be bored with each other, and yet boredom never came, only the further excitement at the prospect of my seeing her again. Every succeeding time I was with her I liked her better, and discovered more in her—new areas of kindness, intelligence, and passion. I lusted for her.

She was not romantic. She was gentle, she was practical, and a little cautious. She had warned me against herself—she told me she was selfish, bossy, opinionated, and possessive. She said, "I'm impossible to live with." But later she stopped talking this way. She said I made her happy. I had known her a month, but I saw her regularly—almost every evening.

We had made love the first night we met, after the ambassador's party, at two in the morning, in distant Stamford Brook. We made love most evenings, always as if we were running out of time. It became like a ceremony, a ritual that was altering us. Each occasion was slightly different and separable, and fixed in my memory. So this continued, both of us burning, both of us expecting it to end.

But we did not become bored—we were now close friends.

I had had lovers, but I had never had such a good friend, and for this friendship I loved her. I didn't tell her—I was afraid to use that word. The sex was part of it, but there was something more powerful—perhaps the recognition of how similar we were in some ways, how different in others, how necessary to each other's happiness.

Love is both panic and relief that you are not alone anymore. All at once, someone else matters to your happiness. I hated to be parted from her. But she was busier than I was! She had just until July to finish her work, and then it was back to the States and her teaching. We lived with a feeling that this would all end soon, but this sense of limited time did not discourage me. I found myself making plans and, in an innocent way, falling in love with her.

It reassured me. I had never thought that I would fall in love with anyone. Then it seemed to me that living with another person was the only thing that mattered on earth, that this solitary life I had been leading was selfish and barren—and turning me into a crank—and that Flora was my rescuer. Part of love was bluff and fumbling and drunkenness. I knew that—but it was the pleasant afterglow of moonshine. The other part of love was real emotion: it was stony and desperate; it made all lovers shameless; and it did not spare me. I was alive, I was myself, only when I was with Flora, and that was always too seldom.

I could not see her on Friday nights. She did not say why, but Friday was out. I had a colleague—Brickhouse, in the Press Section—who told me that after he got married he and his wife decided to give themselves a night off every week—it was Wednesday. Neither could count on the other's company on Wednesday, and neither was expected to reveal his or her plans. They weren't married on Wednesday night. Of course, most Wednesdays were the same—a meal, television, and to bed—in different rooms that night. That was the agreement. But some Wednesdays found Jack Brickhouse on his own and Marilyn inexplicably elsewhere; on other Wednesdays it was the other way around. This marriage, which was childless, lasted seven years. Brickhouse said, "It was a good marriage—better than any I know. It was a good divorce, too. Listen, my ex-wife is my best friend!"

I used to wonder if for Flora it was that kind of Friday, keeping part of her life separate from me. It certainly disturbed me, because I was free most Fridays. I spent Fridays missing her, thinking of her, and wishing I were with her. Perhaps she knew this—counted on it? On the weekends when I was duty officer I did not see her at all.

I had asked her about her Fridays once. I said, "I get it. It's the night you go to your meeting of Alcoholics Anonymous."

I could not have been clumsier. But worry, self-pity, and probably anger, had made me very stupid.

She said, "Do you have to know everything?" And then, "If it is Alcoholics Anonymous I'm hardly likely to tell you, am I? A.A. is very secret, very spiritual, and no one makes idiotic jokes about it. That's why it works."

Maybe she was an alcoholic? But a few weeks later she told me that her father had had a drinking problem, and I knew somehow that she didn't.

Still, every Friday night I seemed to hang by my thumbs. On two successive Fridays I called her at her apartment, but there was no answer. Was she in bed with someone else and saying, "This is our day off"? I wondered whether I could live with her and allow her her free Fridays. But of course I could—I would have allowed her anything!

And from this Friday business I came to know her as someone who could keep a secret. She did what she wanted; she stuck to a routine; she would not be bullied. So, not seeing her on Fridays, I learned to respect her and to need her more, and it made our Saturdays passionate.

She never stayed the whole night with me, not even on the weekends. On the nights when I went back to her apartment she woke me up and always said, "You're being kicked out of bed." It was so that she could work, she said. She was determined to finish her Mary Shelley research on time.

On one of those late nights, when I was yawning, getting dressed sleepily, like a doctor or a fireman being summoned at an unearthly hour—but I was only going home to go back to bed—she said, "By the way, I'm busy next weekend."

"That's okay," I said. But the news depressed me. "What are

you doing?"

Her beautiful silent smile silenced me.

That weekend passed. I missed her badly. I saw her on the Monday, and we went to the movie *Raging Bull*. She hated its violence, and I rather liked its Italian aromas—boxing and meatballs. I took her home in a taxi, but before we reached Stamford Brook she kissed me lightly, and I knew she had something on her mind.

"Please don't come in," she said. "I'm terribly tired."

Well, she looked tired, so I didn't insist. I had the taxi drop me at Victoria and I walked the rest of the way home. It was pleasant, walking home late, thinking about her. And it did not seriously worry me that there was a part of her life that she kept separate from me, because when we were together we could not have been closer. I had never met anyone I liked better. It became a point of honor with me that I did not discuss her absent Fridays or that weekend. It was the only weekend she asked for—there were no others.

Enough time had passed, and we were both committed enough, for us to think of this as a love affair. Flora must love me, I thought, because she is inspiring my love. But so far, the embassy knew nothing about it.

This was just as well. Not long after Flora's mysterious weekend, we were given a talk on the antinuclear lobby in Britain. The feeling was fiercely against our installing nuclear missiles in various British sites. Every party hated us for it—the Labour Party because it was anti-Soviet, the Liberals because it was dangerous, the Conservatives because it was an iniquitous form of national trespass. We knew it was unpopular. We had five men gathering information on it. They had the names of the leaders of the pressure groups; they had infiltrated some of these groups; they had membership lists. They filmed the marches and demonstrations and all the speeches, whether they were at Hyde Park or at distant American bases in the English countryside, where the more passionate protestors chained themselves to the gates.

One of the films concerned a group calling itself Women Opposed to Nuclear Technology. It was not an antiwar movement:

they weren't pacifists: they did not advocate unilateral disarmament. Their aims struck me as admirable. They wanted Britain to be a "nuclear-free zone": no missiles, no neutron bombs, no reactors. And they were positive in their approach, giving seminars—so the boys on the third floor said—on alternative technology.

This film showed them marching with signs, massing in Hyde Park, and demonstrating at an American base. The highlight of this weekend of protest was an all-night vigil, which won them a great deal of publicity. They didn't shout, they didn't make speeches. They simply stood with lighted candles and informative posters. It was a remarkable show of determination, and one of the women in the film was Flora Domingo-Duncan.

I sat in the darkness of the embassy theater and listened to the deadpan narration of one of our intelligence men, and I watched him take his little baton and point in the general direction of the woman I loved.

"This sort of person is doing us an awful lot of harm," he said.

I smiled, and loved her more.

Did she know she was on film?

"No," she said, "but I'm damned glad you told me. The others will be mad as anything. Why did you tell me?"

"It's every citizen's right to know," I said. "Freedom of information."

She laughed. She said, "Now you know about my Friday nights. But I thought that if I told you about it you'd have to keep it a secret."

"It wouldn't have mattered," I said.

"Something else to think about. You're busy enough as it is."

It never occurred to her that I might disapprove of her agitprop because I worked for the U.S. Embassy. It was nothing personal. She had acted out of a sense of duty.

I said, "If I say I admire you for this—acting on your beliefs—will you think I'm being patronizing?"

"You're very sweet," she said. She wrinkled her nose and kissed me. "Let's not talk about atom bombs."

The matter was at an end. Everything she did made me love her more.

We went on loving, and then something happened to London. In the late spring heat, the city streets were unusually full of people—not tourists, but hot idle youths who stared at passersby and at cars. Battersea seemed ominously crowded. They kept near the fringes of the park and they lurked—it seemed the right word—near shops and on street corners. They carried radios. There was a tune I kept hearing—I could hum it long before I learned the words. "Dancing on the Radio," it was called.

> *We start the fire*
> *We break the wall*
> *We sniff the smoke*
> *Which covers all thĕ monsters*
> *Look at us go*
> *Dancing on the radio,*
> *Hey, turn up the volume and watch!*
> *Turn up the volume and watch!*

And there was a chanting chorus that went, *"Make it, shake it, break it!"* It was a violent love song.

The youths on the streets reminded me of the sort of aimless mobs I had seen in Africa and Malaysia. These south London boys looked just as sour and destructive. They lingered, they grew in numbers, and their song played loudly around them.

Flora called them lost souls. She said you had to pity people who were unprotected.

"Then pity the poor slobs whose windows are going to be broken," I said.

"I know. It's a mess."

I said, "All big cities have these little underdeveloped areas in them. They're not neighborhoods, they're nations."

Flora said, "They scare me—all these people waiting. They're not all waiting for the same thing, but they're all angry."

Many were across the road from Overstrand Mansions. They sat at the edge of the park; sometimes they yelled at cars passing down Prince of Wales Drive, or they walked toward the shops behind the mansion blocks and paced back and forth. There was always that harsh music with them.

"If this was the States and I saw those people I'd be really worried," Flora said. "I'd say there was going to be terrible trouble. But this is England."

"There's going to be trouble," I said.

She looked at me.

"We're getting signals," I said.

The boys on the third floor, the ones who had filmed Flora, were now showing us films of idle mobs.

Then the trouble came. It did not begin in London. It started from small skirmishes in Liverpool and Bristol, and it grew. It was fierce fighting, sometimes between mobs—blacks and whites fighting—sometimes against the police. The sedate BBC news showed English streets on fire. It did not have one cause; that was the disturbing part. But that also made it like the African riots I had seen. There was trouble in a town and all scores were settled—racial, financial, social, even family quarrels; and some of the violence was not anger, but high spirits, like dancing on the radio.

When it hit London there were two nights of rioting in Brixton, and then, spreading to Clapham, it touched my corner of Battersea. One Sunday morning I saw every window broken for a hundred yards of shopfronts on Queenstown Road. There had been looting. Then the shop windows were boarded up and it all looked uglier and worse.

I had been at Flora's that night. We heard the news on her bedside transistor, and on the way home I had seen the police standing helplessly, and seen the running boys and the odd surge of nighttime crowds.

I was then deeply in love with Flora. I had been looking for her, I knew. She said the same, and this well-educated woman quoted a Donne poem that began, "Twice or thrice had I loved thee,/Before I knew thy face or name..." But in finding her I had discovered an aspect of my personality that was new to me—a kinder, dependent, appreciative side of me that Flora inspired. If I lost her it would vanish within me and be irretrievable, and I would be the worse for it.

She was different, but that did not surprise me. All women are different, not only in personality but in a physical sense. Each woman's body is different in contour, in weight, in odor, in the way she moves and responds. It is possible, I thought, that every sexual encounter in life is different and unique, because every woman was a different shape and size, and different in every other way. But what about men?

Flora said, "I've stopped wondering about that. 'Men' is just an abstraction. I don't think about men and women. I just think about you and me."

We were at my apartment, one Saturday, sitting on my Chinese settee from Malacca. I wanted to tell her I loved her, that sex was part of it, but that there was something more powerful, something to do with a diminishing of the fear of death. It was an elemental desire to establish a society of two.

"Let's talk about love," I said.

"*Folie à deux,*" she said. "It's an extreme paranoid condition."

There was an almighty crash. I ran to the balcony and saw that a gang of boys had stoned a police car and that it had hit a telephone pole. The police scrambled out of the smashed car and ran; the boys threw stones at the car and went up to it and kicked it. Then I saw other boys, busy ones, like workers in an air raid scurrying around in the darkness, bringing bottles, splashing the car. They set the car on fire.

I shouted. No one heard.

Flora said, "It's terrible."

"This is the way the world ends," I said.

She hugged me, clutched me, but tenderly, like a daughter. She was afraid. The firelight on the windows of my apartment came from the burning car, but it looked more general, like the sprawling flames from a burning city. And later there were the sounds of police sirens, and shouts, and the fizz of breaking glass, and the pathetic sound of running feet slapping the pavement.

We sat in the darkness, Flora and I, and listened. It was war out there. It seemed to me then as if we had been transported into the distant past or future, where a convulsion was taking place. How could this nightmare be the here and now, with us so unprepared? But we were lucky. We were safe and had each other. And, in each other's arms, we heard the deranged sounds of riot and, much worse, the laughter.

Past midnight, Flora said, "I'm afraid."

"Please stay the night," I said.

"Yes. I'm so glad we're together. Maybe we have no right to be so safe. But nothing bad can happen to us if we're together."

Her head lay against my chest. We had not made love, but we would sleep holding each other and we would keep death away.

She relaxed and laughed softly and said, "You didn't really think that I'd leave you tonight. I'm not brave—"

"You're brave, you're beautiful," I said, and I told her how every night that we spent together was special and how, when it came time to part, it hurt and made me feel lopsided. I told her how happy I was, and how many places in the world I had looked for her—in Africa and Asia—and had practically given up hope of ever finding her, though I had never doubted that she existed. All this time the windows were painted in fire, and I heard Flora's heart and felt her breathe in a little listening rhythm. Tonight was different, I said, because we could spend the whole night together—it was what I had wanted from the moment of meeting her. And what was so strange about liking her first of all for her hair and her green eyes? That's how I had recognized her! She had been funny and bright and had made me better, and this nightmare world did not seem so bad now that we were together, and—

"To make a long story short," I said.

And then she laughed.

"Isn't it a bit late for that?" she said.

Born and raised in Massachusetts, the observant and witty *Paul Theroux* now divides his time between London and Cape Cod. He writes short stories, novels, and non-fiction, and his international reputation keeps soaring. He has won the Whitbread Award in England and an American Institute Award in Literature from the American Academy and Institute of Arts and Letters. His story "White Lies" appeared in SSI No. 34.

For readers who can't read...

Greek, Arabic, Chinese, Japanese, Dutch, Norwegian, Chukchi, Finnish, Hindi, Turkish, Urdu, Hebrew, Russian, Vietnamese, Portuguese, etc., etc.

Short Story International takes you to all points of the compass, to anywhere in the world. There are intriguing stories waiting for you in future issues of SSI—stories that will involve you in corners of this world you've never seen . . . and in worlds outside this one . . . with glimpses into the future as well as the past, revealing fascinating, universal truths that bypass differences in language and point up similarities in people.

Send in the coupon below and every other month SSI will take you on a world cruise via the best short stories being published throughout the world today—the best entertainment gleaned from the work of the great creative writers who are enhancing the oldest expression of the entertainment arts—the short story.

A Harvest of the World's
Best Contemporary Writing Selected
and Published Every Other Month

Please enter my subscription to
Short Story International
P.O. Box 405, Great Neck, New York 11022
Six Issues for $22, U.S. & U.S. Possessions
Canada $24 (US), All Other Countries $25 (US)
Enclosed is my check for $_____ for _____ subscriptions.

Name_____

Address_____

City _____ State _____ Zip _____

Country_____

Please check ☐ *New Subscription* ☐ *Renewal*

Gift for:
Name _____
Address _____
City _____ State _____ Zip _____
Country _____
Please check □ New Subscription   □ Renewal

Gift for:
Name _____
Address _____
City _____ State _____ Zip _____
Country _____
Please check □ New Subscription   □ Renewal

Gift for:
Name _____
Address _____
City _____ State _____ Zip _____
Country _____
Please check □ New Subscription   □ Renewal

Gift for:
Name _____
Address _____
City _____ State _____ Zip _____
Country _____
Please check □ New Subscription   □ Renewal

Gift for:
Name _____
Address _____
City _____ State _____ Zip _____
Country _____
Please check □ New Subscription   □ Renewal

Gift for:
Name _____
Address _____
City _____ State _____ Zip _____
Country _____
Please check □ New Subscription   □ Renewal

For the young people in your life. . .

The world of the short story for young people is inviting, exciting, rich in culture and tradition of near and far corners of the earth. You hold the key to this world. . .a world you can unlock for the young in your life. . .and inspire in them a genuine love for reading. We can think of few things which will give them as much lifelong pleasure as the habit of reading.

Seedling Series is directed to elementary readers (grades 4-7), and **Student Series** is geared to junior and senior high school readers.

Our stories from all lands are carefully selected to promote and strengthen the reading habit.

Give a Harvest of the World's Best Short Stories
Published Four Times a Year for Growing Minds.

Please enter subscription(s) to:

____ **Seedling Series: Short Story International**
$14. U.S. & U.S. Possessions
Canada $17 (U.S.) All Other Countries $19 (U.S.)

____ **Student Series: Short Story International**
$16. U.S. & U.S. Possessions
Canada $19 (U.S.) All Other Countries $21 (U.S.)

Mail with check to:
Short Story International
P.O. Box 405, Great Neck, N.Y. 11022

Donor: Name _____
Address _____
City _____ State _____ Zip _____
Country _____

Send to: Name _____
Address _____
City _____ State _____ Zip _____
Country _____
Please check ☐ New Subscription   ☐ Renewal

Send to: Name _____
Address _____
City _____ State _____ Zip _____
Country _____
Please check ☐ New Subscription   ☐ Renewal